Trygve Lindstrom

Tales from Libby, Montana

JIM NELSON

outskirts
press

Trygve Lindstrom
Tales from Libby, Montana
All Rights Reserved.
Copyright © 2024 Jim Nelson
v3.0

This is a work of fiction. Names, characters, businesses, places, events, locales, and incidents are either the products of the author's imagination or used in a fictitious manner. Any resemblance to actual persons, living or dead, or actual events is purely coincidental.

The opinions expressed in this manuscript are solely the opinions of the author and do not represent the opinions or thoughts of the publisher. The author has represented and warranted full ownership and/or legal right to publish all the materials in this book.

This book may not be reproduced, transmitted, or stored in whole or in part by any means, including graphic, electronic, or mechanical without the express written consent of the publisher except in the case of brief quotations embodied in critical articles and reviews.

Outskirts Press, Inc.
http://www.outskirtspress.com

ISBN: 978-1-9772-7156-3

Cover Photo © 2024 www.gettyimages.com. All rights reserved - used with permission.

Outskirts Press and the "OP" logo are trademarks belonging to Outskirts Press, Inc.

PRINTED IN THE UNITED STATES OF AMERICA

Dedication

Although this is a book of fiction, Libby, Montana's a real town where I grew up, where I made lifelong friends and spent much of my time in the Cabinet Mountains, in Kootenai National Forest, and exploring the many nearby lakes and rivers. We had a cabin on McGregor Lake and Mom made what I still consider the world's best meat loaf and cinnamon rolls. Fiction herein often blends with fact. My father was one of the local Libby doctors and his office décor did display (rather hideous) paint by numbers paintings. Some parts of Tryg's life are autobiographical, although I made him far more intelligent and precocious than I could ever hope to have been. The tales are part memory, part imagination, but all a tribute to *the dear hearts and gentle people that live in my hometown.*

This book is dedicated to the good people of Libby, most especially to the Libby High School candle-lighting class of 1963. We still refuse to curse the darkness.

Acknowledgements

Editing! That's where the work takes place. After the fun part is over, the writing, editors find that extra space between words or the misplaced quotation mark. They find "Tryg" where "Conrad" should be; they cross out redundancies. Thousands of errors lurked in my manuscript, discovered by my accomplished editors: wife, Melanie, and best of friends, Joe Nigg. There's a special place in Valhalla for editors.

Table of Contents

1. The Lindstroms Move to Libby (Tryg, age 2) 1
2. A Tale of Two Wasps (Tryg, age 6) 6
3. Tippy (Tryg, age 7)..18
4. Collecting (Tryg, age 7)..27
5. The Snow Fort (Tryg, age 8)...34
6. Sledding (Tryg, age 9) 45
7. The Brown Trout (Tryg, age 10) 50
8. The Fisherman's Story (Tryg, age 10)...........................55
9. A Tale of Two Books (Tryg, age 10).............................61
10. The Cricket Hunter (Tryg, age 11)..............................69
11. Aebleskivers (Tryg, age 11)..82
12. The Smithsonian (Tryg, age 11).................................88
13. The Big Game Hunter (Tryg, age 12)..........................94
14. Ice Capades (Tryg, age 12) 100
15. Tryg on Trial (Tryg, age 13) 109
16. The Ice Tunnel (Tryg, age 15) 118
17. Kingfisher Creek (Tryg, 16).......................................125
18. Jennings Rapids (Tryg, age 18) 132
19. The Mouse and the Spider (Tryg, age 18).................141
20. Tennis Anyone? (Tryg, age 18) 144
21. Muerte Canyon (Tryg, age 27) 148
22. Last Rites (Tryg, age 27)...155
23. Return to Kingfisher Creek (Tryg, age 27)................158
24. Jackson's Dog (Tryg age 65)...................................167
25. A New Adventure (Tryg, age 65)..............................175

1

The Lindstroms Move to Libby
(Tryg, age 2)

Dorothy: *"I'm so glad to be home again!"*
L. Frank Baum
The Wizard of Oz

Dorothy: *There's no place like home.*
From the movie, *The Wizard of Oz*

Conrad and Annika (Anna to everyone) moved from Minneapolis to Libby, with their sons, Trygve and Nicholas, (two and nine years old, respectively) and Sherlock, the family basset hound. They were attracted by pristine lakes and rivers. It was a place where they could afford to buy lakeshore property on sparsely populated McGregor Lake and build a cabin. For Conrad, it was a chance to move back to western Montana, where he had grown up. He needed to move away from the "big city" of Minneapolis, where he had spent his residency and subsequently accepted a position with the prestigious Lowery Hill Medical Clinic. Soon, the Lindstrom bank account was burgeoning, but the doctor wasn't happy. He used to joke with Anna, that he was specializing in diseases of the rich. The more exorbitant the fees, the more exotic the treatments, the more his clients seemed to appreciate him, insisting on ever more frequent appointments for ailments, minor and imagined.

Finally, Conrad shared his feelings with Anna. To his surprise, Anna said she had no interest in driving a Mercedes like the other wives of his colleagues. Nor did she want to purchase one of the grand old Lowery Hill homes, two story red brick with white Corinthian columns and arched double door entrances. She barely tolerated the posh cocktail parties that the senior medical partners insisted they attend, and she most certainly did not want a coat of ermine or mink or arctic fox. If expected to host a cocktail party at their home, she had already decided to serve "honest Norwegian fare" rather than escargot, caviar and similar hideous hors d'oeuvres caterers offered at those oversized mansions. Of course, Anna would have a variety of fish: two or three kinds of herring, lox, lutfisk and smoked salmon. And what a cocktail party be without the most important item: Norwegian meatballs? Conrad was especially fond of Anna's pork ribs. Certainly, there'd be pickled beets and slices of cucumber marinated in vinegar, sprinkled with sugar. Conrad and Anna both burst into laughter imagining how their guests might react to a traditional Scandinavian smorgasbord with aquavit instead of champagne.

Nor did Anna long to return to her hometown, Minot, North Dakota. The only thing she would miss in Minneapolis: attending the glorious Episcopal cathedral with its grand organ and angelic choir. Conrad had underestimated his wife, again.

Conrad started making inquiries. Doctors, he discovered, were in short supply throughout Montana. Bigfork, Polson, Ennis, Dillon, and Libby were all issuing desperate appeals for doctors, some offering to pay for the move, even promising additional monetary incentives. Towns placed ads in newspapers in Spokane, Portland, Seattle and, yes, even in Minneapolis' *Star Tribune*. Sommers had lost its only doctor shortly after its lumber mill closed and the town council was offering to pay a year's rent and utilities on a "ready to move in" three-bedroom home. Larger cities like Helena, Billings, Bozeman and Great Falls placed recruiting ads in major medical journals. Conrad visited several places in western Montana, but settled on Libby, a town built on the magnificent Kootenai river. A town of rivers and streams and lakes. A town with a thriving population and only one doctor.

Anna insisted the move was an escape from Minnesota's legendary mosquitoes. She liked to say that every one of the ten thousand lakes spawned ten million skeeters. Dr. Conrad gave his notice, put up their "starter" home for sale and contacted a Libby Realtor to find suitable office space and a home. He leased the vacant old post office building at the end of Mineral Street, a block from the railroad tracks and directly across from the Texaco station. He found an old but serviceable X-ray machine in Spokane, purchased thanks to their Minneapolis savings account, and soon established a thriving business. Two years later he was able to build a new office building on South Libby Hill, just four blocks from their home.

Mineral Avenue was the commercial street in town, with a restaurant, bar, grocery store, drug store, clothing store, gas station, knitting shop and movie theater. It ran from Highway 2 north to the railroad tracks. The town even had a drive-in theater and an A&W franchise. Saturday's matinee, always packed with kids, featured a double header, serial, and cartoon, all for thirty-five cents. Upstairs was a "cry room," a favorite place for a young couple to be alone until the usher came by. Once a week the milkman read Anna's note on the kitchen door, delivering milk, buttermilk (for Conrad), cream (for Anna's carrots and peas) and butter. He entered the always unlocked home putting items in the refrigerator. Conrad was happy. Anna was happy. The kids adapted readily. Sherlock seemed indifferent; it's not easy reading a basset's emotions.

The great majority of Libby's residents lived in small wood-frame houses or in one of the two trailer parks. Most of the homes were heated by wood-burning furnaces, wood being readily available, and Pres-to-Logs from Libby's K. Swenson Lumber Company were inexpensive. Smaller mills in other towns all had teepee-shaped sawdust burners, to dispose of sawdust waste, but Mr. Swenson turned sawdust to profit. Loggers and miners seemed to have just enough money to pay the mortgage and a car loan but were left with little in the way of discretionary funds. Autumn hunting played an essential role in the community's welfare. Men cooperated in communal hunts where several families agreed to share the spoils: elk and deer venison, and the occasional moose or bear if someone managed to acquire a tag in the hunting lottery.

Conrad soon enjoyed the fruits of the town's economy. In lieu of a burdensome medical bill, a citizen might deliver some elk steaks or a Canadian goose. Conrad's freezer bulged with pickled whitefish and smoked trout; the Lindstroms always had a supply of venison jerky. Autumn brought jars of applesauce, honey, serviceberry jam, loaves of zucchini bread, far too many zucchinis and occasionally a special prize: a pint of huckleberries. The family ate well, but the life of a country doctor wasn't exactly one of creature comfort. When Conrad delivered Leslie's twins, her grateful husband showed up with a paint by numbers rendering of a Winslow Homer painting. Conrad accepted the gift in payment and the word got around. In time, the walls of Conrad's medical office displayed a variety of similar masterpieces: clowns, wildlife, mountain scenes and one painting so poorly done that people debated about the subject matter. Particularly "proactive" patients in the waiting room occasionally found it helpful to rearrange the celebrated painting's orientation from portrait to landscape. Conrad insisted that every painting find a place, even though he harbored an irrational discomfort of clowns.

The Lindstroms soon gained acceptance from most of Libby's citizens, even though many still rankled that Conrad's football heroics at Whitefish High School had broken Libby hearts at the state championships. Anna played the small pump organ at St. Luke's Episcopal Church. Only half a dozen families were members, but they were delighted to at last have music (and another family). Lutherans dominated with a big church and their own school. The Lindstroms received invitations for dinner from each Episcopal family where Anna discovered the weekly bridge club and made a best friend in Nancy Jackson. Libby had only one other doctor, greatly overburdened, who welcomed the newcomers with open arms. Many patients had been driving 90 miles to Kalispell since non-emergency appointments with Doc Holmquist required waiting a month or more. It didn't take long for Doc Conrad's waiting room to be filled; the town could have easily supported a third physician.

Our tales begin when Tryg is six.

2
A Tale of Two Wasps (Tryg, age 6)

You can observe a lot just by watching.

Yogi Berra

In nature's infinite book of secrecy
A little I can read.

Shakespeare
Antony and Cleopatra

Paper Wasps

The Schmidt Pain scale
    0   *No pain*
    1   *Slight pain*   *Paper wasp*
    2   *Painful*   *Bald-faced hornet*
    3   *Sharply and seriously painful*   *Velvet ant*
    4   *Traumatically painful*   *Spider wasp, Bullet ant*

Justin Schmitt
The Sting of the Wild

I've always been fascinated by wasps. They're beautiful, exotic, mysterious and can even be dangerous. They hunt, pollinate, build wonderful nests, often do terrible things to other insects and demonstrate compelling, sometimes disturbing life histories. Unlike poor honeybees whose sting results in certain unpleasant death, wasps are armed with needle-like stingers without barbs so they can inject with impunity their unpleasant cocktail of proteins, peptides and enzymes. When their venom sac is empty, the supply simply replenishes overnight. By the way, I beg to differ from Schmitt's pain scale. From personal experience, I'd say a honeybee's sting might qualify as "moderate pain," and I can attest that paper wasp stings are definitely "painful." I once got stung in the ear by a bald-faced wasp. To me it was somewhere between seriously and traumatically painful. I shudder to think of the pain inflicted by the sting of a velvet ant or spider wasp, insects I keep mounted and displayed, safely dead and mounted in cases under glass.

When I was four, Mother drew the blueprints for a two-bedroom log cabin to be built on Father's bit of lakeshore on McGregor Lake. She apparently decided that she could be an architect and designed our cabin exactly as she wanted it to be. She selected the materials, too: the outside logs from Libby's mill, large picture windows facing the lake, the cobblestone-look linoleum flooring, the interlocking knotty pine boards for the walls, the open beam ceiling. She selected the fixtures and cabinets and appliances from a supplier in Kalispell. A Libby carpenter built our cabin that summer, all by himself, cutting everything with a hand saw. I remember envying his muscles. By my birthday in early autumn, we could sit in the small living room and gaze at the lake through those two large windows. The only source of heat was the fireplace with a fan to circulate hot air. But we had the essential comforts of home: electricity, running water, indoor plumbing.

Almost every Saturday evening throughout the summer we enjoyed fresh-caught trout or hamburgers grilled over charcoal. Father usually arrived from Libby by six or seven after closing the office and picking up Sherlock. Nicholas would have the glowing coals ready. During those warm days of summer, Mother much preferred that Father cook outside where we could enjoy eating outdoors at the picnic table and view the lake. Deer often ventured to the lakeshore in the early evening to drink. We *could have* enjoyed the experience . . . except for the wasps!

As soon as the tantalizing aroma of sizzling trout or ground beef or maybe a venison steak from the freezer wafted from the grill, the carnivorous beasts began circling. Yellow and black-striped demons licked their wicked chops, obsessed with purloining a share of our dinner. Cheeky, bold hymenopterans landed on our plates, pranced across our food, bit a mouthful of protein and dashed away, eager to inform their mates back at the hive that dinner was being served. *Our* dinner! Soon, our picnic table was overrun by wasps circling our heads and diving onto our dinner. Mother was alarmed. Inevitably we'd wave the white flag and retreat into the cabin.

But where was the hive? By the time I was six, after a previous summer of involuntarily eating dinner indoors, I just had to find out. I traversed our back yard, tree by tree and looked under eaves of nearby cabins, trying to find a big grey paper wasp nest. At night I searched by flashlight, illuminating every tree, one by one, all the way to Highway 2, certain that a light grey nest would pop into view. Nothing. I tried to follow the cheeky devils, but they easily escaped my pursuit. They *had* to be close; how else could they appear so quickly whenever our choice of barbecue settled on the grill? Could the nest be farther away, across the highway and up the hill? It seemed unlikely. Then one day while looking for huckleberries just behind our cabin I spied a wasp, and another and another, flying low to the ground around the stump of a fallen tamarack tree. They were disappearing into and emerging from a small hole at the base of the stump!

Did wasps nest underground? I thought they built paper nests, hanging in trees or sometimes in eaves. In fact, I already had a few paper nests in my collection, extracted in the winter when it was safe to collect them. But sure enough, I had discovered something new and wonderful. I sat and watched. Ten or twenty wasps entered or departed the entrance every minute. This must be where they had been purloining morsels of our trout to feed their hungry grubs. I had to know more. I crept closer until I was only a few feet away from the nest. The wasps ignored me, so I sat down and watched. They were industrious as honeybees at a hive. Oh, if I could only view inside that small opening to observe the nest. How could I safely excavate the opening and look inside?

An ice-fishing pole! Perfect! We had two telescoping bamboo ice-fishing poles that could be extended to 18 feet. When the sections collapse, an ice fishing pole is about six feet long and maybe an inch and a half in diameter. We used them on the Kootenai, standing on the shore and extending the poles over the ice shelf to open water. Maggots are the preferred bait for whitefish, kept in the refrigerator in a container of paper shavings. Mother hated the thought of maggots, much less maggots in our refrigerator. But somehow Father had cajoled her into that huge concession. We'd thread a single maggot on a small hook with a lead shot weight and drop the hook into the current. Oh, the bitter cold we endured, standing for a couple of hours, a steady breeze usually blowing upstream. But we were usually successful in catching several whitefish delivered to the Rogstads who smoked or pickled them, returning half to us. Nicholas refused to join our ice fishing ventures, insisting that bait fishing was beneath the dignity of a true fly fisherman.

Luckily the fish poles were in the cabin where Father was planning to apply a fresh coat of wax to them in preparation for winter. Sherlock, our sedentary basset hound, lay at Father's feet, snoring peacefully, occasionally uttering subdued staccato howling noises as he dreamed of chasing rabbits or foxes or maybe a cute, *similarly inclined* female basset. Sherlock spent most of his life sleeping, interrupted by short bouts of eating and his involuntary daily walk. I never saw him chase anything, not even a squirrel. Father insisted our hound join him on a daily walk, accounting for Sherlock's entire daily exercise regimen.

The cabin now smelled of huckleberries as a pie in the oven announced, "I'm almost ready." Mother sat at the kitchen table busy solving a NY Times crossword puzzle and enjoying Nat King Cole's crooning "Smile though your heart is breaking" on our well-worn LP record:

Our eclectic record collection at the cabin included Belafonte, Tom Lehrer, Shubert's Trout Quintet, Beethoven's nine symphonies and assorted cello pieces. I still remember the lyrics to every Tom Lehrer song. Preparing for my wasp encounter I sang to myself, "*If you're looking for adventure of a new and different kind. . . .* Oh yes, I was looking for adventure.

Nicholas was working on his latest project, selecting his very finest dry fly of each kind for a display in a wooden case, lined with black velvet. What a boring display it was becoming. He started with a grey fly, he called it the Hendrickson, supposed to look like a mayfly. (I knew better than to point out that it didn't look much like a real mayfly). Next to the Hendrickson rested a gray fly with a bit of blue on the body. Then came a gray fly with a touch of dull yellow. On and on the procession of flies took their places, perfectly aligned along the taut sewing thread. Perfection, thy name is Nicholas. He held up his latest masterpiece, a pure black Griffith's Gnat. Father assured him that it was the most perfect gnat he had ever seen. (Nicholas managed the slightest smug smile). When Nicholas couldn't find a copy of a fly meeting his standard of perfection, he left a space; he'd create a better one back home in Libby. One fly might have white wings; the next looked exactly the same, except sprouting wings of black. His grand plan was to display 160 flies and then have a printed "key." Not a single resplendent royal coachman in the entire display. I decided I was going to make my own display box (I could use a cigar box) with a royal coachman in the center, a showy orange salmonfly on one side and a Joe's grasshopper on the left, all creatively asymmetrical. I had recently caught an ichneumon wasp, 8 cm long if you count the ovipositor. I'd put it in the display box as well. My friends would love it. Nicholas would *hate* it!

Yes, the inside of our cabin was a tableau of domestic tranquility, a modern-day Vermeer painting. When I retrieved the fishing pole, Father gave me a quizzical look but said nothing, accustomed I suppose to my quirky behavior. Just another typical Lindstrom Saturday. I saw no reason to explain what I was doing. Mother would have disapproved.

I returned to the nest, proud that my persistence had finally been rewarded and determined to make a thrilling scientific discovery. I likened myself to Carter opening King Tut's tomb, preparing myself to exclaim, "Wonderful things!" I settled down in a safe prone position some 15 feet away and quietly, carefully extended the four telescoping sections. Could the wasps hear me? I made a mental note to find out about how insects hear things. Tom Lehrer would have been proud of me: I wasn't nervous, flustered or scared. I was prepared! My plan was to probe the wasp nest entrance with the tip of the pole. The wasps would never figure out that I was the intruder. I was far away from the nest. I was as still as a log. I lay on my stomach edging the pole forward, closer and closer to the underground hive. The wasps continued to enter and exit normally, unaware of my approaching excavation. I couldn't help but admire my ingenuity, my triumph of scientific intellect over primitive instinct. As the tip of the pole crept forward, now just inches away, I hesitated. Some self-preservation part of my brain was trying to get my attention. "Stop!" the voice said. "Danger!" it shouted. (The voice sounded like Mother). I ignored my brain's cowardly advice. Carter *had* to enter the tomb and I *had* to excavate this new discovery. I boldly plunged the pole, soft earth falling away, the opening now the size of a fist.

Hubris, thy name is Trygve.

I believe "all hell broke loose," can appropriately be used here to describe what happened next. A terrifying hissing black and yellow snake suddenly emerged from the hole, rearing up like a cobra. Only it wasn't a snake; it was a solid plume of wasps. Very grouchy wasps. The snake morphed into a miniature tornado, hundreds of small warriors circling angrily, looking for the intruder, their hissing crescendoing into an ominous electric buzzing. Not to worry, I was 15 feet away, lying on the ground. I did my best to make myself small, to resemble a log. The tornado descended onto the offending pole; then the host of enraged Amazons began advancing down the pole, the pole I was still holding, the pole which unfortunately was pointing directly at me!

"Run!" The self-preservation part of my brain screamed. This time Mother's voice had my full attention. "Run" now seemed like an excellent idea. I leapt to my feet and dashed back toward the cabin, pursued by a cloud of hellions, bombarding me with hot, terrible stings. Should I have dropped to the ground and rolled around or does that work only when a person's on fire? Maybe I could have run past the cabin and dived into the lake. I was eagerly awaiting instructions, but my self-preservation brain was now distressingly silent, having clammed up after the monosyllable, "Run!" I was screaming something inane like "ahhhhhh" as I jumped onto the back porch, burst through the door and ran into the cabin, wasps in hot pursuit.

I was still yelling as I raced through the living room. Anna started screaming. Sherlock woke up howling and scrambled for cover under the bed. Conrad found a broom and started swatting, knocking the record player to the ground with a crash, Nat King Cole rolling across the floor and shattering into pieces. Nicholas crouched in the corner, his flies scattered across the floor. I ran into the bathroom, still yelling, and jumped into the shower, wasps still clinging to me. The cabin was filled with dozens of intruders for Father to deal with. Mother huddled down at the kitchen table, hands over her head, terrified and crying.

So much for domestic tranquility.

Meanwhile, while I was drenching myself in the shower, ankle-deep water now began pouring onto the bathroom floor, the shower drain clogged with drowning wasps.

Black huckleberry-scented smoke began pouring from the oven.

By some miracle, Mother, Father, Nicholas and Sherlock all escaped stings; I suffered 17. Each turned into a quarter-sized red welt. My face took the most hits, cheeks, ears, neck, nose. One eye was swollen shut. My lower lip was fed and swollen. The sharp pain lasted for an hour, unmitigated by ice and baking soda. Throbbing dull pain persisted for two more days. Sherlock couldn't be persuaded to emerge from under the bed until Father opened a can of Alpo, his favorite treat. A basset soon forgets trauma when offered food.

Mother let me stay home from church that Sunday. My swollen face would have startled her friends. Several years later I wrote a poem, trying to capture the moment.

Mother's in the kitchen sobbing;
"Nat King Cole's" kaput.
Sherlock's howling under the bed;
Our pie is black as soot.

Nicholas, with a pair of tweezers,
Retrieves his dry flies from the floor;
He never liked me very much;
He now dislikes me even more.

(I lined dead wasps in the living room.
Some drowned, some smashed with Father's broom.)
Forty-two wasps in our cabin are dead;
I lined them up from left to right.
My eye is swollen shut and throbbing;
Oh, the chaos, oh the fright!
With a burst of laughter Father said,
"Just a typical Saturday night."

The pain has gone; my face has healed.
The record player's been replaced.
But it's going to be a long, long time,
For these memories to be erased.

How I wanted to restore the peace;
Tranquility my fervent goal.
It has taken several years
To atone for Mother's tears;
(Or deserve another cinnamon roll).

Despite my injuries, I just couldn't give up on that nest. When Mother, Nicholas and I returned to the cabin the next week, I was armed with "Kill 'em Dead!" wasp spray from Libby's drug store. I returned to the scene of the crime, sprayed the nest thoroughly and excavated the hole to discover dozens of dead wasps and, to my surprise, a paper nest, complete with hexagonal cells filled with (now dead) grubs. Dozens of wasps returned to their home, repelled by a lingering white film and Kill 'em Dead fumes. I suppose they found another place to live. I only regret that I couldn't find the queen. She would have been a trophy fit for her own wooden cigar box.

Mud Dauber Wasps

It was now midnight and my task was growing to a close. I had completed the eighth, the ninth and the tenth tier. I had finished a portion of the last and the eleventh; there remained but a single stone to be fitted and plastered in. I struggled with its weight and placed it partially in its destined position.

My heart grew sick; it was the dampness of the catacombs that made it so. I hastened to make an end of my labour. I forced the last stone into its position. I plastered it up.

Edgar Allan Poe
"A Cask of Amontillado"

The next summer, Mother asked me, again, if I had put away my sled and skates. I've never been much good at putting things away. Nicholas, by contrast, excelled at placing all things in their proper place. Once in a while I'd tilt Mother's favorite painting ("Sailboat on the Fjord") and try to be around when Nicholas entered the living room. He *always* checked that painting and made sure it was level again. He had an elaborate erector set with screws and pieces of metal, gears and tiny nuts and bolts and small electric motors. I never had the patience to bother with assembling a model. But he built all kinds of cool things like a powered steam shovel and a biplane complete with spinning propeller. I always asked him to keep them out for display, but at the end of the day, he'd take his creation apart and put each piece back into its proper spot in the original box. He probably thought I'd play with his creations and ruin something. Come to think of it, he did have a point.

I remembered that Mother had asked me, more than once, to put away my winter things. But at the time I had been busy doing boy things like making a rope swing and watching water striders in the little creek behind the house. But Mother was now standing in front of me, arms folded with "that look" that brooked no more procrastination. I didn't see anything wrong with keeping sleds and skates in the garage, but I knew better than to dispute Mother-with-folded-arms.

Nicholas and I sleep in a bedroom on the second floor, a converted attic. Part of the attic was unimproved, a space behind a small door, where we stored our Christmas lights and decorations, sleds and skates. Sheets of plywood over the rafters make it safe for walking. As I put my sled next to Nicholas,' I spied a wasp at the far end of the attic where it could enter through a hole in the vent. What a magnificent wasp it was: impossibly narrow, nearly 5 cm long. I went back to my bedroom and gathered up a flashlight, journal and pencil, hoping the wasp would still be there.

When I returned, I moved the light across the sloped roof and discovered something wonderful, a mud nest the size of a softball visited by two wasps. Mud daubers! Jet black with yellow-striped legs. My flashlight did not seem to bother them at all. There were several small holes at one end of the reddish-brown clay nest. As I watched, another wasp arrived, holding a motionless spider. What wondrous thing was I watching? The wasp disappeared into a hole and the backed out again without the spider. The attic was already getting uncomfortably warm, but I stayed as long as I could stand the heat. One wasp was making a new cell with little dabs of mud. Another arrived with a spider. Wasps were filling mud cells with spider after spider. Finally, I watched as a wasp closed the entrance with a final dab of mud. It was time to go; I was feeling faint in the heat and thrilled at my discovery. I knew I had to return during the coolness of early morning.

I raced downstairs just as Father was returning from a long day at the office. After dinner, he would leave again for an hour or so to "do his rounds:" visiting any of his patients who were in the hospital.

I gathered the family together to give them my spectacular news: we had mud dauber wasps in the attic! Mother looked alarmed. Nicholas rolled his eyes. But Father smiled and assured me that all of us (giving a particularly stern look toward Nicholas) would listen, *respectfully*, to what I had to say. The radio was just about to shut down for the night, closing, as always, with Kate Smith singing:

Without a song the day would never end,
Without a song, the road would never bend,
When things go wrong a man ain't got a friend,
Without a song.

Radio silenced, I launched into my enthusiastic observations. Father was the only one who showed an interest, Mother fearing the danger of an infestation of wasps. Later that night, after Father returned from rounds, he asked me to take a seat next to his wingback chair. He was holding a book. "Son," he said. I want to read you one of my favorite stories. Your mud dauber observations reminded me of it. It's called, 'The Cask of Amontillado,' by Edgar Allen Poe. By the way, amontillado is a kind of expensive wine," he explained.

From then on, I've always associated Poe's story with mud daubers. Every year I read the story to my grad students at Harvard.

I watched those lovely wasps for hundreds of hours over several summers, taking notes in my journal. Over that time, I found three other nests, one a single cell, the others small adobe "apartment buildings." Never did a wasp bother me or seem disturbed by my presence, even though I often sat just a few inches away from a nest. That Christmas I learned more about mud daubers, when Father gave me a wonderful book: *Fabre's Book of Insects*. Fabre taught me about how the wasp lays a single egg in each cell. Then she (the female wasp is the hunter; male bees and wasps have no stingers) paralyzes a spider before placing it into the mud cell. Fabre was filled with wonder at the perfect precision: the spider has to paralyze the spider without killing it. So, the injection has to be perfectly placed in the spider's nerve center, with the precise amount of venom to paralyze without killing. If the spider regains mobility, it will thrash around in the cell and kill the newly hatched grub. If the spider dies, it will soon become a moldy, rotting carcass polluting and killing everything within the cell. When the cell is full of spiders, the wasp seals the chamber. The wasp egg hatches into a tiny grub that devours the living, paralyzed spiders which are helpless to move and confined in utter darkness. Finally, the grub spins a cocoon and in time emerges as an adult wasp which chews through the sealed doorway.

Fabre quickly became my hero, a largely self-taught entomologist from France who learned by watching and experimenting. I hadn't worked out that the spiders were still alive. I still have never seen the drama of a mud dauber hunting and paralyzing a spider. But I did make my own discoveries. One strange thing I saw was that if a wasp dropped a spider before she managed to deposit it into a cell, she simply abandoned her quarry she had worked so hard to capture. It would have been so easy to follow her prey to the attic floor and retrieve it.

One day I saw a second, smaller wasp flying around one of the nests. When the mud dauber left, the smaller wasp entered the cell for a moment. What was she doing? I had an idea: I bet she's laying her own egg in the cell! Years later I learned about the cuckoo wasp that does exactly that, her grub hatching out ahead of her rival, devouring the mud dauber egg and then dining at leisure on the spiders meant for her rival.

3
Tippy
(Tryg, age 7)

The perpetual ideal is astonishment.

I have never separated the writing of poetry from prayer.

Derek Walcott

The good thing about living in a small town is that people pretty much know everything about everybody. The bad thing about living in a small town . . . of course you can finish the sentence. We all know each other, for better or for worse. We know who gets mean when he drinks too much at The Blue Bear. We know who brought an elk to the butcher without a hunting tag, not that anyone cared. We all understood: it meant winter meat for families. We know whose kids get free lunches at school and whose dad had to leave the Little League baseball game for yelling at the ump. We know who showed up with a fishing lure in his ear at Doc. Lindstrom's house (he claims his wife made a careless cast). Someone have a chimney fire or get a ticket for speeding? Expect the news to appear in our weekly paper *The Libby Logger*.

Need an auto mechanic? That'd be Alvin Cooper. Unless you're willing to drive 90 miles to Kalispell, a "big" town, Alvin's your man.

Don't like his politics or religion or the prices he charges? Too bad. It's Alvin, or do it yourself, or make the 90-mile drive on Highway 2 with no guarantee the bill will be any less. The town's too small for Lutherans to quarrel with Roman Catholics or Methodists. Towns of a certain size survive only if the folks find a way to get along with one another. We've got one grain store, one gas station, one pharmacy, one place for breakfast and lunch, and one bar and grill. So, we're forced to adapt, make compromises. Forgiveness, or maybe a degree of discomfort, or at least a requisite tolerance for compromise is a small town's imperative to survival. I suppose it's not much different for families; Nicholas and I managed to tolerate each other.

Libby's citizens tend to avoid controversial subjects like politics or religion. We've all got our opinions and are unlikely to change. Our town is a collection of characters, each one with their story. I guess we're not much different from other towns. Take some time to get to know a person and you'll discover something memorable, or despicable, something evoking sympathy or admiration or disgust; sometimes you might even unearth a tale of heroism. Would you believe that quiet, gentle Sven got two purple hearts in the Big War. Two! He's got a big scar across his abdomen though it takes a lot of coaxing before he'll show you. Sheila successfully performed the Heimlich maneuver on her son, probably saving his life. The obstructing cherry Life Saver (lovely irony, that) flew out of little Tommy's mouth like a cannon ball. She keeps the candy in a jar with all of Tommy's baby teeth. Why keep the teeth? You'll have to ask her. 'Course the "Heimlich maneuver" hadn't even been invented yet. I prefer to call it the "Sheila Maneuver."

When Caspar was a junior in high school, he got awfully sick--scarlet fever or something. Ben tutored Caspar on the phone, for an hour or two, five nights a week for six months while Caspar was bed-ridden. Caspar graduated from high school on time with the rest of us. All 79 of us graduated that year, the biggest graduation class ever. To me, Ben's one of our quiet heroes. It's taken me a long time to appreciate that our town was filled with wonders.

One "wonder" was Tippy. I wish I had taken the time to learn more about him. Occasionally, Tippy would come to town. He wasn't, strictly speaking, a *town* character. I don't think Tippy actually had a town to call home. He'd just arrive from time to time like a Gypsie. We all sort of adopted Tippy and I guess he sort of adopted us. As far as we were concerned, he was one of us. He'd park his rusty pick-up at the end of Montana Avenue and knock on the door of all the houses (avoiding Martha White, of course. She had a great big sign on her front door that read: "NO SOLICITING!" and she meant it!). Martha was the town grouch, a retired high school math teacher whose husband had worked in the lumber mill. On warm days, she'd sit on her porch and just watch people. If you said, "Hi," she'd just stare at you, not answering. Spooky. We kids avoided her house even on Halloween. One year someone (we all know who did it, but no one's squealing) posted "NO TRICKS OR TREATS" next to her NO SOLICITING door sign.

Back to Tippy. My friends and I just couldn't stop gawking at Tippy's pickup truck. Judging by a few latent bits of paint, it had once been dark blue. All four fenders had rusted through, rattling back and forth as if ready to succumb to gravity at any moment. We "Five Rangers" placed bets--dibs on any dud baseball card--on when the first fender would actually fall off. I don't know what attracted us to the old thing. There's nothing unusual about trucks in our town; More than half the men drive a pickup. Maybe it was simply the sheer oldness, the improbable fragility. Maybe it was our conviction that Tippy was somehow mysterious and so was his truck. There was an old pillow on the driver's side covering exposed springs. You could see the pavement through a small hole in the floor by the brake pedal. But the main attraction of Tippy's derelict vehicle was the wonderful camper, a motley collection of boards of various faded hues, and rusting sheet metal.

"Found every piece of wood myself," he'd announce proudly. "All I had to buy was some nails. You should see all the things I find lying in a dump," he continued.

"You boys should go treasure hunting at the Libby dump. 'Course the smell is pretty bad. Here's a good trick: I put Vick's Vaporub under my nose and wear a bandana. I have a hoe for moving stuff around and wear gloves that I boil afterwards. There's lots of ravens and seagulls flying around finding stuff to eat. Found a dead cat once, covered with maggots. 'Shoulda seen the maggots falling all over each other. I went back a few days later--thought it'd be cool to have a cat skull, but I couldn't find it. Prob'ly buried under new garbage."

How clearly I remember our excited grimaces and groans . . . and how much we loved hearing those gruesome details! Oh, how we wanted some kind of animal skull. Tippy told us about how to cut off the head, boil it in a pot of water, scrape off the hide and then leave it in the sun for a few days.

"I've found old blue and green medicine bottles," Tippy continued. "People'll pay a quarter each, and folks throw away rusty tools that just need a bit of cleaning, and old wooden windows with a perfect pane of glass. I even found a cast iron frying pan and a tin coffee pot that I use every day. Be sure to look for old radios and get the bulbs. People collect them."

We Five Rangers loved these stories. For sure we were going to ride our bikes out to the dump. We'd especially love to have an animal skull! We'd be sure to carry a sharp knife and a flour or gunny sack to put the head in and of course we'd wear gloves.

The camper had a peaked roof just like a little house, with boards instead of shingles. Tippy was wonderfully proud of his hand-built little house. It even had a little window that he could open (probably recovered from some dump). Oh, how we looked forward to stealing a glimpse of the treasures that must be inside his camper!

Tippy sharpened things. I suppose there must be a name for his occupation, but we could never come up with one. He sharpened carving knives and scissors, axe blades, lawnmower blades and chain saws. Whenever Tippy was in town, the news went out. When he came during our summer vacation, our Five Rangers gang of boys would hop on our bikes and pay Tippy a visit. He provided our entertainment for a few days.

The back end of the camper had a door as wide as the tailgate. Tippy would open the door, pull out a ramp and then lower his wagon with the large wooden toolbox. "Here's where the magic happens," Tippy loved to say. Tippy would then pull his wagon up the street (The only sidewalk in town was on Mineral Ave.) and stop at each house. Mama Ingebretson (we called her Mama, because she had 11 children) always had a few things for Tippy to sharpen. Better yet, she always handed him a lovely loaf of fresh-baked bread. Under the counter of Mama's kitchen was a great big flour bin on rollers. Mama seemed to always be baking and handing out thick slices of bread to us kids. At the end of the day, Tippy always shared his loaf with us. We'd all break off a hunk of Mama's bread. Sometimes, one of us might manage to go home to borrow some honey or huckleberry jam.

At the end of the day Tippy let us count his day's earnings. Tippy's cash register was an old wooden cigar box with a hinged lid. The lid said, "Habana Gold" and there was a green tobacco stamp on it. When he returned the knives and scissors to the owners, he handed the customer the cigar box. People could pay whatever they deemed fair. Starting pay at the lumber mill was a bit more than $2 an hour, so we figured that $10 was a pretty good day just for sharpening stuff. One day we counted $14.71, which included a silver dollar dated 1898. Back then you could get silver dollars at the bank, anytime you wanted them.

With a couple of scissors and a few knives in hand, Tippy would set up shop, right there on the side of the street, sitting on his little red wooden bench. On hot days, he'd find a nice shady spot under a ponderosa. He seemed to enjoy having an audience of curious boys. When Tippy opened his magic toolbox, we always gasped on cue with wonder: flat files, round files, polishing stones, even a small stone wheel. He taught us about wrenches: Allen wrenches, open-ended wrenches, crescent wrenches. He had Phillips and slotted screwdrivers, a heavy vise and his own "secret formula" sharpening oil. I can still recall the smell of that oil.

Tippy would carefully file a blade for a while, and then gingerly apply his thumb to the edge, as we winced, afraid he'd draw blood. Then he'd file just a bit more. Finally satisfied, with a showman's flourish, he'd slice a piece of paper to our appreciative oohs and aahs. Once Tippy filed my fishin' knife for me. I was so proud of the razor edge. When Tippy returned my knife, shining like it was brand new, I put two quarters in the tip box, my week's allowance. A box of 50 Remington .22 shells cost exactly fifty cents, so I had to postpone target practice that week. Best fifty cents I ever spent.

As Tippy advanced along Montana Avenue toward South Libby Hill, some of us would race home to let our parents know he was coming, hoping they'd find something that needed to be sharpened. Many of the men in town were proud of their sharp axes and chain saws. "Don't think we'll be needin' Tippy this year," they'd say. But we rangers were persistent.

"What about scissors?" we'd ask. "Mom's been complaining how dull they are." Yes, Tippy had his little band of curious onlookers but we were also pretty good at drumming up business. The most important thing that Tippy did each fall was to sharpen the blades on our sleds and ice skates. Tippy spent a good hour on each one and waxed them too. We could hardly wait for the first good snow to race down South Libby Hill. My father was always a pushover. I could count on him to let Tippy sharpen our lawnmower and scythe and mom's scissors and anything else I managed to scrounge.

After a few days in town, Tippy would pack up and leave, his truck spewing blue exhaust, coughing pitifully, fenders flapping like undersized wings but still managing to cling to the truck's body. We'd have to place new bets whenever he decided to return. Before he left, we had our little routine. We helped him with his grocery shopping: he'd stock up on things like coffee and beans, bacon and oats and sugar at The General Store. Then we'd all go to The Three Mountain Goats Café for breakfast. Tippy'd order huckleberry pancakes and two fried eggs, bacon, crispy hash browns and coffee. Marcie always had real huckleberries, fresh or fresh frozen, "Not that compote stuff," she'd say. Most of us just got a mug of hot chocolate for a dime. Coffee was only a nickel, but we didn't like coffee much back then. We always felt a bit sad to see Tippy leave town. We knew it would be months before he returned.

We were kind of afraid to ask Tippy personal questions, but Tippy liked talking and taught us lots of stuff. He'd say, "Always eat the skin of trout, 'cause there's lots of good nutrition in the skin. But never eat the liver of a bear. It'll poison you. If you get a mosquito bite, press it hard with a fingernail, make a line right across the red mark and it won't itch." One day he told us that every person, if they live long enough, does at least one very special, heroic thing in their life. If you really want to know someone, find out about that special thing. From then on, I wanted to find out more about people. And I wondered what heroic thing each of us might accomplish.

Of course, we all wanted to know what heroic thing Tippy had done. Sandy just couldn't help himself: he asked Tippy, "Did you ever do a special thing? Maybe sharpen a king's sword?" he added hopefully.

Tippy laughed and laughed at that and all us kids started laughing as well. Funny thing, laughing. Sharpening a king's sword seemed like a pretty good question. Back then I couldn't see what made it funny. But Tippy's laughter was contagious, so we all had a huge, good laugh for no good reason. Finally, Tippy said, "I'm pretty sure that a king must have his own personal sword sharpener. He'd have lots of servants to polish his boots and take care of his horse and such. (That sounded reasonable to us). But maybe I did one really good thing when I was about your age."

Half a dozen boys waited anxiously to hear his story.

"You boys know Kingfisher Creek?" he asked.

Of course, we did. At least we had heard the stories. In a few years, when we turned 16 we knew that we had to backpack to the creek and spend the night. If you live in Libby, you don't officially become a man until you've spent the night at Kingfisher Creek. We were expected to catch a trout and cook it for our dinner, and sleep there under the stars. Don't even *think* about sneaking back to town before morning! I've been there twice. It's maybe the prettiest place I've even seen, with a waterfall and a pond and the creek and all. It's where I met Moira.

"Well, Tippy continued, "Karl Swenson himself was offering five dollars to a couple of strong young boys to carry a special backpack to Kingfisher Creek. Can you guess what was in them backpacks?"

We had no idea.

"Fish! Little bitty rainbow trout about three inches long. Each backpack had five gallons of water just packed with little fish. Fingerlings they called 'em. Good world for 'em; 'bout the size of a man's fingers. Five gallons of water is pretty dang heavy. I reckon each backpack weighed about 50 pounds. But Olie Jackson figured we could hike up to Kingfisher Creek. Heck, it's only a bit over four miles. And we was mighty happy to earn a whole five dollars. All we had to do was empty the container into the pond and then come back.

"Mr. Swenson drove us and our bikes to the trailhead early one morning and let us out. He said that we could ride our bikes back home. We took off together with all that weight on our backs and we didn't stop a single time to rest 'til we got to the creek. It took more'n two hours, but we made it and we was mighty proud of ourselfs. Just a couple of boys doing man's work and getting paid. When I was a boy," Tippy continued, "there was no fish in the creek or in the big pond. Mr. Swenson bought the fish from the hatchery. I guess it was kind of a gift to our town. Now you know a special secret: how Kingfisher Creek got rainbow trout."

The next summer we waited for Tippy. He never showed up. We all tried to get information, but no one seemed to know anything. Was he dead? Maybe he was hurt or sick and in some hospital.

Sometimes in the summer we'd ride our bikes to one of our favorite spots on the Kootenai, or Libby Creek take a nice swim and just lie around and talk. Tippy was often the topic of conversation. Where does he live? Where does he go to the bathroom or take a shower? Does he sleep in his camper in the winter? Did he ever marry? Does he have kids? We never found out, but all these years later we still remember Tippy. That fishing knife Tippy sharpened many years ago occupies an honored place in my cabinet of curiosities.

JIM NELSON

From my journal, *Poems for Posterity*

Tribute to Tippy

When Tippy opened his magic box
Enthralling our gang of boys,
He somehow opened up our minds
To simple, homespun joys.
He taught us to respect our tools
And keep things in repair,
(Although his rusty, derelict truck
Spewed smoke into the air.)
He taught us like a father,
Lessons that have not ended.
Thank you, Tippy, wherever you are,
From the boys that you befriended.

4

Collecting
(Tryg, age 7)

The world is full of magical things waiting for our wits to grow sharper.

Bertram Russell

Already reading at age four and writing my first poems at five, I had frequently and impatiently implored my parents to let me advance to a higher grade or perhaps let Mother school me at home. Finally, I called a "family meeting" and delivered a short lecture.

"I know I'll be the smallest kid in my class. I'm no good at sports. I'm the slowest runner. I know that in a way I don't belong with older kids. But I'll *hate* being in the third grade. For sure I don't belong *there*. Have you seen the books they read! I *have* to be in the fifth grade!"

I had come prepared. I had a copy of our third-grade reader, a book called *Just Imagine*. I turned to a story in the middle of the book and read a page:

Mother and Father both laughed when they saw Long-Tail.

"He's not a kitten," said Father. "He's a baby squirrel. He fell from his nest in the tree and his mother did not find him. But he may stay with Puff, because she thinks he is a kitten."

Then Dick thought of something funny. "Oh my," he laughed. "What will Puff think when he wants to live in a tree?"

I saw my parents trying their best not to laugh. Victory was mine. They just *couldn't* inflict the third-grade version of Dick and Jane on me.

Mother and Father agonized over my increasingly insistent request. They discussed the issue with teachers and the principal. Everyone had reservations. But they knew I had already read every *Oz* book in the library *Pinocchio* and *Alice in Wonderland*. Now I was reading Father's boyhood favorites: Terhune and Jack London and Robert Louis Stevenson. For the second year Libby's librarian had allowed me to check out Holland's *The Butterfly Book* and *The Moth Book* for the entire summer. No one else had checked them out for several years. I was already starting my third poetry journal. Conrad gently reminded Anna that I already had four best friends in the fifth grade, friends who lived on Montana Ave: the other Four Rangers. Conrad himself had started college at 16, earning his MD at 24.

"My friends don't care if I'm little," I continued. "Especially if they can come over once in a while and get a cinnamon roll. I may be the smallest, but I'm going to be big one day. Father's six foot five! Mother's five foot eight! I just need a little time to grow bones and muscles. By the time I'm in college, I'll be tall and maybe I'll even be able to run fast!"

Anna reluctantly joined the other decision makers in measured approval. I was promoted to fifth grade just before my eighth birthday. I was the shortest boy in the class, the last chosen on the baseball team at recess. But I didn't care about sports. I spent my "bench time" finding treasures like click beetles. I even convinced some of the younger children to bring me specimens. In time, half a dozen kids from the elementary school gathered around me at recess and I taught them about bugs. I especially enjoyed placing a click beetle upside down and delighting my students when the beetle catapulted two feet into the air. I showed them where to find cecropia cocoons and how to recognize ground beetles. They learned to watch bees without fear and soon they recognized sweat bees and bumble bees. They knew the difference between dragonflies and damselflies. They knew that flies had two wings and bees had four. They found ladybug larva, delighted to know what they had found. In the summer, my little army, each equipped with nets of muslin that Mother had fashioned, started bringing me butterfly specimens. I needed more cigar boxes.

One thing we boys had in common: we collected things. Otto liked to walk along the railroad tracks and pick up rusty spikes. They were about five inches long. He already had 12 spikes in his collection. We all kept our eyes peeled and brought them to Otto to negotiate some kind of trade. We all thought his collection was pretty terrific. Nobody asked why he wanted them; collecting anything was worthy of our respect. Marv had a really great collection: coke bottles. The bottom of the bottle is stamped with the city and state where the bottle was made. He wanted to see how many different cities he could find. Sam collected glass telephone insulators. He started his collection after he found two in the Libby dump, nice green ones. After that he'd trade marbles or baseball cards to anyone who had an insulator. He now has five, my favorite being a small blue one stamped "MADE IN U.S.A."

All of us collected baseball cards. For five cents you could buy five baseball cards and a stick of Bazooka bubble gum from Topps, all wrapped up in a colorful wax paper container. The gum was a thin wafer the same size as a baseball card, a brittle wafer that often was broken into a few pieces. Almost all the baseball cards were "duds," our label for players we didn't know. We actually knew only a few names: Mickey Mantle and Hank Aaron, Sandy Koufax and Willie Mays. But we never got the famous ones. Not a single one of us, who had collectively bought hundreds of cards, had a "keeper," like Mickey Mantle. We all felt kind of gypped. We kept our cards in a box (usually a shoebox). Jonson (he pronounced his name Yonson) collected New York Yankee cards and he'd always give two of his dud cards for a Yankee player. He said he'd give his entire collection for a Mickey Mantle. We all said we'd do the same. But even Jonson had, as far as we were concerned, a box of duds, Yankee duds.

Alex used to tell us that old baseball cards could be really valuable. He said a Babe Ruth card could be traded in for a nice brand-new car. Of course, we all laughed at that, but we figured we could at least get a brand-new bicycle, maybe even new bicycles for all of us Five Rangers. Every one of us talked to our parents and grandparents to see if they had any old baseball cards, but none of us had success. Guess we'd have to keep our old bikes. Funny thing: at our 10-year high school anniversary, I asked the old gang about their shoeboxes of baseball cards. Not a single one of us, including me, had saved those cards. Maybe a few weren't duds after all, but we'll never know.

Another thing we all collected: marbles. We all had our sack of marbles: clearies, cat's eyes, aggies, a couple of thumpers and maybe even a steelie. I suppose "collected" isn't quite the right word. We all had an accumulation. We had our favorites of course. We never gambled with a favorite. My treasure was a large blue and white marble, kind of bumpy, that had been my grandfather's. New marbles are always perfectly smooth. I'd never trade grampa's thumper or risk losing it in one of our marble battles. We carried around our marbles for combat. In the fall we'd bring our marbles to school to play "Tick Wins." First, we flipped a coin. The winner always started by dropping a marble (we played on the sandy part of the playground where marbles stuck where they landed). Marbles get lost in the grass and they roll too far on the hard dirt. The loser then took three giant steps from the marble and became the shooter. The shooter aimed at the target (marble #1) and almost always missed. Even Ben, our best Little League pitcher almost always missed. The other player now became the shooter, picking up his marble and taking two giant steps away from the other marble (marble #2). From two steps away, bending over and aiming, you had a pretty chance of "ticking" the target marble. If successful, the marble was yours. Otherwise, the process continued from only one step away--pretty much a sure shot. The loser started the next game.

On a really bad day, you might lose three marbles, but fortunes of marble warfare went back and forth. We all knew the rules, passed down year after year. For more excitement, you might choose a really nice aggie and challenge someone with a red cat's eye (rare) or even a steelie (a ball bearing). You could agree to surrender several ordinary marbles if your aggie lost. Sometimes we'd trade marbles. A red or blue or green clearie could be worth quite a few cat's eyes. Everybody had lots of cat's eyes. We called big marbles "thumpers." No one wanted to lose a thumper, so if you had a thumper battle (high drama, that) and your thumper got ticked, be prepared to give up a few marbles from your bag.

Another game involved a circle in the sand about a yard in diameter with two or three marbles in the middle. The younger kids made a smaller circle. Shooters then shot their marble by flipping it with a thumb. Hit a marble, it's yours. Miss and you lose. Tick Wins was a lot more exciting. We'd play marbles every recess in the fall until the first snowfall.

Quite a few of us tried collecting stamps for a while. For a dollar you could order a whole pound of stamps on paper. First you had to soak the squares in warm water and ease off the stamp. Next you had to let the stamps dry. The stamps tended to curl up, so we put them under a book or cookie sheet to dry. It was too much work. There were way too many duplicates. You could buy stamps off paper, of course, but they were twice as expensive. Or you could get a bunch of stamps in envelopes "on approval," really nice sets, but none of us could afford that.

Maxwell's Worldwide Stamp Book at the drug store cost two dollars, but it turned out to be pretty worthless. The United States had only ten pages. We'd never get the great old stamps pictured on the first five pages. Germany had four pages. Half the rectangles on each page had a picture of a stamp; the other rectangles were blank. We affixed the stamps with stamp hinges--five cents for 100. Most of the time, the glued stamp went on a blank space, because we couldn't find the right picture. And then, what do we do with all the duplicates? Everyone had the same crummy duplicates.

Most of the stamps were easy to identify. Norge of course was

Norway. Deutschland was Germany. But there were always some mysteries. Luckily our county library had a set of six big paperback books called *Scott Standard Postage Stamp Catalogue.* There was a "key" for difficult stamps like Japan or China. One of the books, the *specialized catalogue* was just for the U.S. On page 4 was the first U.S. stamp, catalog number 1, a five-cent stamp with Ben Franklin's portrait. Used: $300! Mint: $3,000! Number 2 was a ten-cent stamp that said "X cents X" on the bottom and had George Washington's portrait. Used: $700. Mint: $12,500! You could buy a house with that mint Washington stamp. These wonderful books showed a picture of every stamp in the world! And they showed the value of each stamp, used or mint. Of course, all our stamps were used. And not a single stamp was worth more than three cents, if we could ever find a buyer. We all grew tired of stamps. Getting really good stamp books cost a lot of money. And the stamps we really wanted cost a lot more money. Baseball cards were cheap and railroad spikes were free!

 I was the most prolific collector of all of us. My bug collection was just part of my little natural history museum. I had bird nests (even a lovely little hummingbird nest) and wasp nests and even a fungus collection. Whenever we went to Spokane or Kalispell, I implored my parents to visit a rock shop. Usually, I was able to leave with something beautiful. I loved fool's gold and little geodes, obsidian, agate and copper ores like azurite and bornite. One Christmas we visited my father's sister, Aunt Freja, in Mill Valley, California. She gave me my first seashell, a Venus comb, and that started my seashell collection. It's still my very favorite. Whenever I walked in the woods, I looked for fungus on rotting logs. Some are really beautiful, especially when shined with oil. I had a foot long sugar pinecone that my aunt sent me from California, several moth cocoons and an ostrich egg that my brother (would you believe) Nicholas gave me for Christmas. What I really needed was a display cabinet.

 I guess you could say I was also starting a book collection. Mother had been an English teacher while Father was in medical school; she gave me her books on poetry. Father gave me his dog books by Terhune and adventure books like *Robinson Crusoe* and *Treasure Island* and *Call of the Wild*. Each year I added a book from Duncan's in Spokane. The other Rangers think it's stupid to collect books that are in our library, but they don't understand the pleasure I feel, surrounded by books. Today, every bookshelf in our home is crammed with books, floor to ceiling. Two cabinets of curiosities now overflow with, well, curiosities. I've got green obsidian, tarantula fangs, preying mantid egg sacs, my father's brass microscope. But I don't have a single baseball card or marble, not even my grandfather's blue and white thumper.

5

The Snow Fort
(Tryg, age 8)

Snow had fallen
Snow on snow, snow on snow

Christina Rosetti
"In the Bleak Midwinter"

Tryg felt warm air blowing from the furnace vent. Nicholas, as usual, had arisen early, descended into the basement, chopped a Pres-to-Log into one-inch slices and built a cozy fire in the furnace. Tryg grudgingly gave his brother credit. Tryg hated getting up early, especially in the cold. Overnight, the home temperature had plummeted. When truly arctic temperatures arrived, someone (the three men of the house taking turns) had to get up every couple of hours to place another Pres-to-Log on the coals. No one wanted to wake up again to frozen water pipes and finger-needles of frost creeping from the windows onto the walls.

With the early-morning chill abating, Tryg stretched and yawned, throwing off his heavy wool blankets in a heap. On the other side of the room, his brother's bed, predictably, was perfectly tucked and folded, pillow centered, linens smoothed. Tryg looked out the second story window to a wonderful discovery: snow! It must have snowed all night--big, heavy fluffy flakes. Two feet deep at least and it was still snowing hard. And fog! Dense fog that often hugged the Kootenai River had crept across the entire valley. Mixed with smoke from the mill and hundreds of wood-burning home furnaces, fog now completely obscured the neighbor's house across the driveway.

Tryg showered quickly and slipped into jeans, leather boots, heavy wool sweater, stocking cap and hooded parka. He was eager to embrace the exciting whiteness. Outside, he sank into three feet of heavy virgin snow, perfect for making a snow fort, he thought. Not the dry powder snow that fell in tiny flakes on sub-zero days and crunched underfoot like baking soda--this was big flake snow, snowball snow, snowman snow, easy-packing wet snow, fort-building snow, 25-degree snow. Tryg caught a few flakes on his tongue, fell over backwards to make an angel and then reentered the house, shaking and stomping snow on the carpet.

Anna was in the kitchen making breakfast. Nicholas was already at the table with his usual two eggs sunny side up and two pieces of toast, one buttered and the other spread with huckleberry jam. "Eggs and toast OK for you?" Anna asked.

"Yes, thanks, Mom," Tryg replied. "Did you see the great snow we're having, and can you believe that fog?"

"Weatherman Steinberg says we might have five or six feet," Nicholas said. "That's all he's talking about on the radio."

"Yea!" Tryg responded. "Looks like we'll be shoveling snow off the roof."

"They've closed down Highway 2 from Kalispell to Bonners Ferry, "Nicholas continued. "Whitefish, Polson, Troy, Bigfork and Bonners Ferry all closed school today. Our principal said that Libby had never closed school for weather, even when it was 25 below, and he saw no reason to do so today."

"Where's Father?" Tryg asked, suddenly changing the subject.

"He's at the hospital. Seems Erika Jenholm is actually going to have her baby this time," Anna laughed. "Apparently third time's a charm," she laughed again.

Tryg, with the familiar confusion of amusement and annoyance, watched his brother perform his ritual delicate operation on his eggs. First, he'd carefully eat the white of the eggs until only the yolks remained. Then came the delicate operation of lifting the thin outer layer that surrounded the yolk. Success! The yolk remained intact. Nicholas finally dipped a corner of the buttered piece of toast into the yolk. Nicholas always saved the jam-covered toast and glass of milk for last. Just as his older brother left the table, Tryg's breakfast arrived.

"Why is Nicholas so . . . so different?" Tryg asked.

Anna stifled her laughter. "How many kinds of butterflies are there?" she asked.

"Thousands," Tryg answered without hesitation, trying to decipher his mother's question.

'How many beetles?" she continued.

"Wow. Nobody knows for sure--hundreds of thousands. Maybe a million. There are more species of beetles than all other insects combined. More than all the vertebrates and invertebrates." Tryg realized he was starting to take over the conversation on a favorite topic and forced himself to wait for his mother's Socratic questioning.

Remember the hymn, "All Things Bright and Beautiful?" she asked.

"Of course," Tryg said, beginning to wonder if his mother was going to reach a cogent conclusion. Tryg could always count on Conrad to answer a question directly. Anna preferred a labyrinthine approach, one with twists and turns but always ending at the inevitable destination.

"Well, I think God loves diversity. Things great and things small. Birds and maybe a million kinds of beetles, and trees and elephants--all of it. Think how boring it would be if there were only one kind of dragonfly. At least you wouldn't need so many cigar boxes," she laughed. "Same with people--we're all different, each one of us. Your bed always looks like a tornado paid a visit to your half of the bedroom. Nicholas' bed--you can't tell he spent the night in it. Nicholas arranges his books by height. You, well, your books have an interesting randomness. A few are even upside down. I have no idea how either of you finds a particular book. Your display shelf has seashells, pinecones, your father's old brass microscope and a variety of feathers. Nicholas has four immaculate wooden tall ships arranged, of course, tall to short. It's hard to believe you two are related. If I had a third son, he'd probably sleep on the floor and run off to join the circus.

"You spend hours in the attic watching mud dauber wasps," she continued. "Know anyone else who does that? Nicholas attaches tiny strings to miniature wooden tall ships and makes his own fishing flies. You write poetry; he spends hours on mechanical drawings. Nicholas takes ten minutes to eat his eggs, about nine and a half minutes longer than you take. Your brother has a crew cut, every hair in place. You're more the shaggy dog type. You're both weird and wonderful. Nicholas will probably end up being a banker or a CPA or some kind of engineer; you'll probably be a poet or an entomologist or something else you haven't yet discovered. Oh oh. You better get your books; time to leave for school. Carry them under your coat, it's still snowing hard. Nicholas must be a couple of blocks ahead of you by now."

"Bye, Mom." Tryg blurted. "I've started thinking that *I* might run away and join a circus." Tryg laughed as he gathered his books, barely able to zip his parka over them, bolting outside with a loud slamming of the door.

Already another half a foot of snow! Tryg was delighted. He'd have no problem convincing the Five Rangers to meet on Saturday to build the best-ever snow fort. If necessary, he'd promise cinnamon rolls and hot chocolate. The fog seemed even denser, edging in tint from gray to a sickly yellowish beige. Tryg shuffled through the deep snow to the road and waited. He turned around slowly, taking in the utter whiteness, the silence, the impenetrable fog. Three blocks away, Zeke had started walking down Montana Street. A few houses later Zeke met up with Toby and his black lab.

Two boys and an exuberant dog now plowed through the drifts until Robbie's dim shape came into view through the fog. Finally, the trio spotted Tryg emerging from the fog, the penultimate ranger in line. Sherlock stayed indoors. He did not like the snow. He did not like exercise. He did not frolic. Even on warm days, when the boys and assorted dogs walked to school, Sherlock curled happily on his favorite rug, enjoying a nice long after-breakfast nap. Four boys now marched toward the school, taking turns being the leader, (the one who had to work the hardest, acting as snowplow) following the path Nicholas had created. Two blocks later they joined Otto, the pastor's son, whose blue-eyed husky pranced in joy to see the lab. The reunited Five Rangers and two romping canine companions marched the final three blocks to school. By the time they got to their lockers, their frozen "stovepipe" jeans had begun to soften. The girls, also wearing jeans under their skirts, had to take off their jeans before going to class. Tryg said a silent "thank you" that boys didn't wear dresses and leggings.

By late morning the storm had doubled in intensity. Libby recorded a whopping 76 inches in a single storm. Weatherman Steinberg, also the local radio's disc jockey, station manager and sportscaster for Libby's high school games, called it the worst snowstorm ever. The Five Rangers enjoyed making fun of the Whitefish Wimps, although a "snow day" would have been a great opportunity to get a head start on their planned fort. Instead, they spent Friday looking wistfully out of school windows and making plans for the weekend.

Every Friday Tryg's seventh grade teacher Mrs. Grace had her class write a short essay. Without fail, the class groaning, Alex would ask how long the essay had to be. Without fail, Mrs. Grace frowning, said 250 words would be acceptable. Alex predictably managed, with a triumphant flourish, to insert his final period after the 250th word. The class enjoyed a moment of laughter when Mrs. Grace warned Alex against his last week's sentence, which she shared with the class: "I have never before, ever, seen such a very, very, very beautiful sunset." Tryg didn't bother to count words. His ideas seemed to poise in a sprinter's crouch, eager for the starting gun. Today Mrs. Grace, radio-inspired, wrote the topic on the blackboard: "The Worst Snowstorm Ever." Tryg felt compelled to alter his essay's title to "The Best Snowstorm Ever." He mentioned how much fun it was to shovel snow off his roof and then jump into the deep drifts that reached nearly to the gutters. He enjoyed seeing everybody in town working together. He could not refrain from mentioning the Whitefish Wimps who were probably now sledding or ice fishing on Whitefish Lake. But best of all, Tryg boasted that Saturday the Five Rangers planned to build a spectacular snow fort in his family's back yard, thanks to the best snowstorm ever (nice ending, that, he thought).

Recently, he had decided to end each weekly essay with a poem. That way he was sure to have at least one poem every week to enter into volume three of *Poems for Posterity*. Last week's contribution:

Sunset
By Trygve Lindstrom

Dogs are good for fetching and petting;
The sun is setting.
Mother's doing dishes in the sink;
The sky's turning pink.
Father's outside, enjoying a smoke,
Hearing frogs croak.
Our neighborhood fox has five little foxes,
I need more cigar boxes.
My homework is finished, I'm finally done
And so is the sun.

Mrs. Grace seemed to love Tryg's poetry, always praising his efforts. But Tryg discounted his teacher's uniformly encouraging comments. He longed for some helpful suggestions, maybe some (not too negative) criticism. Somewhere he hoped to find a mentor. Was there such a thing as a creative writing teacher? When Tryg took his sunset essay home, he nearly refused to transfer the poem to his journal. "What a stupid, stupid poem," he mumbled. "What do frogs have to do with sunset, or foxes and cigar boxes? Mother doing dishes . . . terrible!

Trying to rhyme sink and pink. Dumb, dumb, dumb." He labored over the words and finally entered a shorter version into his journal:

Sunset
By Trygve Lindstrom

Sleepy sun is setting, sky golding and pinking.
Her beauty fades quickly, each moment of sinking.
My day's work is finished; I'm finally done;
Soon I will be dreaming, just like the sun.

Better, he thought," pleased with alliteration in the first line. although uncomfortable with "golding" and "pinking. He enjoyed making up words. Mother said Shakespeare had invented more than 200. Was it OK to make the sun female? How many poems before I'm poet laureate; probably at least a thousand? And when will I write something good enough that someone will print it? Even *The Libby Logger* declined his submissions.

He concluded the current week's essay with:

The Snow Fort
By Trygve Lindstrom

The Rangers Five, we're kind of short,
So you'll be amazed when you see our fort.
With buckets of snow, we'll build a wall
And we won't stop till it's six feet tall.
We have a ladder and buckets of snow;
You can watch as we build it; you can watch our fort grow.
It's the best thing ever the Five Rangers have tried.
As soon as we're finished, we'll invite you inside.
All the neighbors will know that we're smart and we're clever
To build the best fort from the best snowstorm ever.

Libby's roads were fairly quiet for several days after the monumental snowfall. Front-loaders scooped snow into the mine's huge dump trucks, which emptied hundreds of loads into the Kootenai. The occasional four-wheel drive vehicles venturing into the white wonderland had bright cloths tied to the top of the antenna, alerting cross traffic of each other. Doc Conrad and both nurses managed to navigate to the office, opening right on time and most patients managed to keep their appointments as the storm finally abated, fog lifting. Weatherman Steinberg promised a sunny Saturday.

Two excited dogs met the Five Rangers as they left the school at the end of the day. At 3 p.m. the sun was already low on the horizon. Many homeowners were already creating avalanches as they shoveled deep drifts from the roofs. Tryg noticed that Mr. Skaags was working on Martha White's house. Martha the grouch! There'd be no fort building until every roof was shoveled, but the boys were exultant: all that extra snow they'd have!

Saturday morning the Five Rangers began arriving at the Lindstrom home. Weatherman Steinberg was talking about some damn fool logger named Jackson who had brought in a full truckload of lumber just before the mill closed for the day. Then came the familiar jungle that always preceded Saturday's Half Hour of Spirituals:

Put another nickel in
In the nickelodeon
All I want is having you
And music, music, music.

Tryg hurried to finish his breakfast and blurted, "Oh Mom, I kind of promised the guys cinnamon rolls and hot chocolate."

Anna laughed. "You start building your fort. I'll call you all in for lunch."

Tryg raced out the back door with the others, shouting, "Let the construction begin."

For three solid hours five boys built their fort, ten feet by ten feet exactly, Alex marking off the precise dimensions with measuring tape. "I bet Nicholas would love a little brother just like Alex," Tryg thought. The boys had managed to scrounge three empty five-gallon buckets that worked perfectly. The snow was heavy with moisture and packed wonderfully into the buckets, making solid cylinders. Overnight the fort would freeze into an ice fort that lasted two months. They had a five-foot tall open doorway and used a handsaw to carve out two windows. Over the top of the doorway, they laid boards, adding a final layer of snow on top. They achieved their goal of six-foot walls, lifting heavy buckets up the stepladder, but what about a roof? Otto came up with an idea. What about covering the roof with a big canvas tarp? Great idea! Conrad had a 12' by 12' green tarp the family often took camping. It would be perfect. A few two by four studs inside the fort created a kind of tent and a heavy layer of packed snow on the walls held the tarp in place.

Five exhausted boys cheered.

Oh, we were boys of winter.

Boys of sleds, toboggans, and ice skates.

Boys of ice fishing, soon to become winter hunters.

Boys of snow forts and snow angels and fierce snowball battles.

Boys aglow with rosy cheeks and noses.

Boys cocooned in gloves and scarves, boots and parkas and home-knit woolen stocking caps.

We were the boys who built that snow woman that Pastor Jenkins found objectionable. We removed the offending features, forever after treasuring with delight the memory of her creation.

We were boys of arctic winds and frozen jeans.

Boys catching snowflakes on our tongues, shoveling deep snow from rooftops and joyfully leaping into the snowdrift's embrace.

Boys who began to feel a vague counter-intuitive sense of discomfort or regret, or loss or sorrow with the coming of longer days, as icicles melted and great chunks of ice started drifting downstream in the Kootenai.

Yes, we were boys of winter.

Alas, we grew into men. Men of spring and summer and autumn. Men who no longer heard the sirens of winter.

Anna watched from the kitchen window, marveling at the boys' energy and enthusiasm. For the umpteenth time, the radio aired the newest advertising jingle. Anna was sure every person in Libby could sing the lyrics:

Give him Doctor Ross Dog Food.
Do him a favor.
It's got more meat
And it's got more flavor.
It's got more things to make him feel the way he should.
Doctor Ross Dog Food is doggone good.
Woof.

Nicholas advised Tryg that if his poet laureate ambition fell short, he might get a job writing advertising jingles.

Conrad had been happy to supply the tarp and some scrap lumber, but otherwise, let the young men work on their own. He would have enjoyed joining the work crew or at least offering some helpful advice. From time to time, he'd wander outside to casually smoke his familiar bent pipe and watch the progress.

"Lunch!" Anna called out the back window as five pink-cheeked, snow-covered, half-frozen, exultant boys rushed into the warm, steamy kitchen, the room filled with the confluent aromas of cinnamon and brown sugar and yeast. Five mugs of hot chocolate, topped with whipped cream and cinnamon, greeted the young corps of engineers. In the center of the table, sat a cake pan with a dozen sizzling cinnamon rolls, Anna lacing them with frosting. Beside the rolls, a meat loaf, hot from the oven. Meatloaf and cinnamon rolls! Tryg's absolute favorite. Lunch fit for a king! What love he felt for his mother at that moment! Tryg had often watched Anna hand grind the beef and veal and pork, crush Zweiback crackers into crumbs, add powdered mustard, salt and pepper and a bit of cream. Conrad watched in dismay as rolls and meatloaf disappeared.

Five Rangers devoured the best-ever lunch in celebration of the best-ever snow fort built following the best-ever snowstorm.

6

Sledding
(Tryg, age 9)

The Child is father to the Man
And I could wish my days to be
Bound each to each in natural piety.

William Wordsworth
"My Heart Leaps Up"

Montana Avenue is a dozen blocks long from South Libby Hill to Highway 2. Northbound, down the long hill from the Lindstroms, and just across the highway lie the elementary, middle and high schools. Southbound, Montana Ave rises to South Libby Hill where kids sled all winter. Most Saturdays the Five Rangers and a dozen other neighborhood kids raced down the steep hill and marched up again, over and over until dusk. Every kid carried a lunch pail with a thermos of hot chocolate or cider and a sandwich. Zeke's mom always packed some raw broccoli that ended up under a bush. Halfway down the slope, the Five Rangers had built a ramp of snow that had turned to ice overnight. Daring sledders could race onto the ramp and go airborne for a few feet before thumping abruptly back to the ground. The landing was exhilarating if a bit jarring. Little kids avoided the ramp, warned by older siblings. Our community of kids looked out for each other. Most of the time there wasn't an adult in sight.

Early Saturday morning, Tryg woke with a start. He vaguely remembered dreaming about snow and sledding. He turned on the light and opened his notebook. He felt a poem anxiously waiting for him. Thankfully, Nicholas was still sleeping. His big brother *did not* like to be awakened. Tryg began writing:

Snow

Far, far away . . . and long ago
A winter storm began to snow
It snowed all day and through the night
By morning everything was white
Snow on roofs of every home
Every fencepost was a dome
Snow on trucks and cars and bikes
Snow on hikers, taking hikes.
We kids all cheered the snowy day
Time to bundle up
And play!

After breakfast we got dressed
In our wooly socks, and vest,
Scarves and knitted stocking caps,
Warmest coats and extra wraps,
Boots with fur as soft as kittens,
Earmuffs and a pair of mittens!

Then we ran outside with joy;
Every girl and every boy.
Some are sledding on the hills,
Laughing when they had their spills.
Some made angels in the street;
Some made pictures with their feet.

We made snowmen, tunnels, forts;
We invented winter sports.
And all the children, every one
Caught falling snowflakes on their tongue

We played all day; our noses glowed
And still it snowed,
and snowed
and snowed!

He fell asleep, pleased with himself.

Saturday was a perfect day for sledding; cold, but sunny with no wind, and several inches of fresh snow. After a hearty oatmeal breakfast (with plenty of brown sugar), Tryg grabbed his sled, thanked Anna for preparing his lunch pail and started walking up the hill, which was already bustling with kids, several older ones daring to try the ramp. Tryg joined the queue walking up the path to the top. He'd show the others how to jump the farthest!

As Tryg prepared to make his first run, Alex arrived with a younger boy, perhaps six or seven. "Hey Tryg," Alex called out. "This is my cousin Stevie Benson. He lives in Dillon. I borrowed Otto's sled for him to use."

"Hi, Stevie," Tryg said. "Looks like the run is really fast today. Why don't you and Alex go ahead. I'll be right behind you."

Stevie lay down on the sled. He looked small on Otto's sled; his boots didn't reach to the back end. Alex gave him a shove and then made a running start to follow, Tryg joining the trio. The hill was indeed fast, with a layer of ice under fresh snow. In the best of conditions, sleds don't steer very well (toboggans are even worse) and don't maneuver well at all on ice. As the three boys picked up speed, Alex and Tryg saw Stevie edging to the left, heading straight for the ramp.

"Go right, go right," Tryg and Alex both yelled.

Stevie did his best to turn the steering bar, but the sled was now careening at full speed and turning ever so slowly. On a shorter sled, he could have dragged his feet to slow down. Little Stevie was going to hit the ramp! Worse yet, his left runner hit the right side of ramp; the sled leaping airborne, throwing Stevie off his sled directly in front of Alex. Tryg watched in horror as Alex ran over Stevie's hand. Seconds later all three were lying at the bottom of the hill, Stevie screaming as blood splattered the snow. Other kids started screaming and crying; Annie threw up. Dogs barked; younger kids cried. A dozen kids ran to the site. Tryg looked at Stevie's hand--it looked bad. The blade of Alex's sled had run across the back of his hand. Three bones were showing. Stevie kept screaming. Alex looked dazed, lying next to his sled.

Tryg picked up Stevie and put him on his own sled. "You be brave," Tryg said. "Hold on. I'm taking you to a doctor." Then Tryg started running down the hill, pulling the boy, leaving a thin trail of blood behind on the snow. Four short blocks later, Tryg arrived home, picked up Alex from the sled and carried him to the front door. He managed to enter his home calling, "Father! Father! Come quick!"

Moments later Dr. Lindstrom was numbing the wound with Novocain and began putting in the first of a dozen stitches. Stevie finally had stopped screaming as Conrad placed a gauze pad over the sutures and wrapped the hand in gauze. "You're lucky, son," Conrad said. There are no arteries in the back of your hand. You've got a nasty cut, but none of your bones are broken. I'm going to give you a shot; don't want that hand getting infected. Your hand's going to be mighty sore for a few days; I'm going to put your arm in a sling. You need to keep your hand elevated. Now I'd like to talk to your parents."

"They're back home, in Dillon, sir, I mean doctor."

"Let's call them now, shall we?" Conrad said smiling.

Tryg went to the front door to let his friends know Stevie was OK. A dozen kids had been waiting with varying degrees of curiosity or anxiety. An open door suggesting an invitation, everyone tumbled in at once. Jill exclaimed, "Oooh, there's blood on the floor."

Anna ushered the kids into the kitchen where she started making hot chocolate. A few minutes later Conrad and Stevie emerged from the bedroom, a makeshift emergency room, Stevie proudly showing off his bandaged hand and sling.

A few weeks later Conrad got a letter and a large carton from Mr. Benson with a check and an offer that the doctor just couldn't refuse: "Dr. Lindstrom. Thank you for taking care of my son. The stiches are out and he's healing nicely. He hopes his scar will stay; something to show off to his friends. He's having a great time telling a quite dramatic story of getting run over by a sled and bleeding all the way to your house. Please come fish the Madison on my ranch. I've got a nice stretch of private riverfront. Mid-June would be ideal; that's when the salmon flies hatch. I hope you enjoy the Angus tenderloin steaks from my ranch."

Conrad sent a letter to Mr. Benson and marked next year's calendar for a June trip to Dillon with his two sons.

7

The Brown Trout
(Tryg, age 10)

Glory be to God for dappled things . . .
For rose-moles all in stipple upon trout that swim;

Gerard Manley Hopkins
"Pied Beauty"

She was a survivor. Surviving hadn't been easy. A prodigal number of her relatives had perished, victims of outrageous fortune's slings and arrows. Predators lurked around every bend. On her first day dozens of her brothers and sisters had fallen prey to opportunistic aquatic insects: predaceous diving beetles and hellgrammites. Specialized spiders had even descended below the water surface to snare helpless newborns. Hungry young fish patrolled the shallows, gobbling the tiny hatchlings.

Her ancestors, introduced from Europe, had adapted well to rivers and lakes across the United States and Canada and even to Australia and New Zealand. The brown trout, *Salmo trutta,* has been welcomed as a desirable game fish rather than an invasive species and has prospered.

She lived, eluding a host of dangers and grew wary and wise. The persistent clear and present danger for a young trout had been larger fish. But escaping into the shallows exposed her to other threats: diving kingfishers and blue herons.

Osprey and bald eagles dived with merciless talons and deadly accuracy. Fish cannot see the plummeting feathered rockets that crash into the river. She learned to stay safely submerged during the day. White pelicans drifted in fishing flotillas. Otters hunted in packs. Bears, red in tooth and claw, stood in the rapids as mature fish swam upstream to spawn. Still, she had survived for 25 years, thirty pounds of muscle, needle-sharp teeth, a mouth that could easily engulf a 10-inch fish. She was now a formidable 35-inch predator endowed with piscine memory, some form of survival intelligence.

In her world, a middle-sized Montana river, she was a monster trophy fish. In 2013, the remains of a giant brown trout had been discovered on the banks of the Madison. Experts determined that "Megasaurus Dino-Brown" (so-dubbed by the newspapers) had been perhaps 34 pounds. But no one had ever actually caught a fish that size on the Madison. A 15-pound brown or cutbow or rainbow caught on the Madison made the front page of fishing magazines, but 30 pounds? The stuff of a fisherman's dreams. She now patrolled several miles of river with near impunity, claiming the darkest, deepest pool as her own. In the winter, she drifted downstream to the reservoir. Realistically only two enemies could now threaten her, a bear at the annual spawning or human beings armed with cruel hooks, wading along the banks or drifting in dories.

No, her life hadn't been easy. A long white scar from an osprey's talon told the story of one close call. Her ragged dorsal fins told another. Yet she had survived, and she had learned.

Twice she had escaped the barbed hooks of artificial flies. The first had torn from her tender young jaw. The wound quickly healed and now she knew to avoid clever weapons of feathers and fur attached to a nearly invisible leader. She now ignored artificial temptations: the multicolored silver doctor and the royal coachman, the black spider and the hare's ear, the elkhair caddis and blue-winged olive, the parachute adams, royal wulff, woolly buggar and the pale morning dunn. She had seen them all and more, drifting past her discerning eyes. Sometimes she followed an offering, mocking the fisherman's stratagem, turning away only when approaching the shallows. Fishermen on the Madison know how hard it is to entice ten-pounders. Trophy fish survived because they were experienced, smart and wary.

Her second encounter with treachery, a dozen years ago, had been more traumatic. Every June, the salmon fly hatch (*Pteronarcys dorsata*) provides an orgy of feasting for a dozen species of fish. The soft bodied flies, nearly two inches long, were an irresistible opportunity for fish to gorge on the bountiful gift of protein. For a few days, myriads of salmon flies skimmed the river's surface, females depositing eggs. The river roiled and churned as thousands of fish, leapt into the air in a joyful bacchanal. In the frenzy, larger berserker trout often rose from the river depths to gulp the smaller ones--easy pickings. The fortunate few fishermen given access to these blue-ribbon waters stood in wonder at the annual extravaganza, the swirling cloud sometimes casting a dark shadow as a bright orange blanket of insects blocked the sun. The roar of splashing fish sounded like a waterfall. Fly rods arced back and forth, propelling lines into the melee, catching a fish with nearly every cast. Overhead, legions of opportunistic swallows darted and dived with abandon into the cloud of insects. Almost every captured trout was released again. With something like religious reverence, fishermen praised their sport as "catch and release." Unless . . . unless they could land something truly legendary, something worthy of a taxidermist.

Suddenly, careless of her danger, she was securely hooked by an artificial salmon fly.

Already 20 inches long, a ten-pound trophy to be sure, the mighty fish raced upriver, tugging against the terrible single-barbed hook, now embedded firmly in her jaw. She dove deep into her favorite pool, only to feel the constant terrible pull of the fisherman's line. Downstream she dashed, leaping in the air and shaking to escape the barbed terror, but nothing could stop the relentless line from drawing her nearer and nearer to shore. She fought with every ounce of her strength, but after half an hour of heroic struggling, her strength began to ebb. As she was coaxed toward shallow water, she could now clearly see her nemesis, a ten-year old boy, reaching a hand toward her as she now lay passively on her side, exhausted, gills struggling for air.

The boy reached toward the gaping mouth avoiding the row of sharp teeth and started lifting her out of the water by the leader, eager to show his brother and father; an excited boy's youthful error proved to be her salvation. With one last frantic burst of energy, she snapped her body in a violent spasm and the leader broke. She fell back into the shallows and raced toward deep water.

Years later, the man vividly relived his boyhood experience whenever he lifted his bamboo flyrod.

The salmon fly remained in her jaw for several months, hook slowing rusting. The attachment was little more than an annoyance, causing no pain, until one day it simply dropped to the bottom of the river. A small scar. She healed. Another lesson learned. Never again would she leap for salmon flies. Instead, every June she feasted on the school of salmon fly larva swarming toward the riverbank, preparing to climb out of the water and morph into creatures of the air.

Despite her skills and knowledge and impressive size, she had nearly been caught a third time, when she was nearly 20 pounds, already a legend to those claiming to have seen a huge shadow moving along a deep bank. She spotted a flash of gold that dropped into her pool, moving with sudden jerks. Impelled by irresistible hunting instinct, she overcame the retreating victim with a single burst of energy and grabbed a shiny brass quarter ounce Mepps spinner, wicked treble hook embedded in her upper jaw.

Few fishermen on the Madison fish with bait or lures. It's illegal, but much more importantly, it violates "the code." For miles, at occasional fishing access points, posted signs announce: "Fly fishing only!" or "Catch and release only." She had never seen a Mepps spinner and grabbed the shiny weapon without reservation. Now she was again forced to fight for her life and a grand fight it was. Her luck held this time thanks to the logjam at the far end of Farley's Pool. The logjam was a favorite fishing spot where a fisherman could move halfway across the river on ancient logs and then cast upstream. Flies floated gently toward the deep pool in front the logjam, enticing arctic grayling which favored the spot.

The logjam was supported by ancient, submerged logs, a perfect sanctuary of hiding places. Into the logjam she swam, charging through ancient openings as other fish scattered. The line soon tangled on gnarled roots and twenty pounds of fury easily pulled free. Another escape. Another page in the legend of the great brown. Another story told in taverns and discounted by other patrons.

Winter was now approaching. A thin layer of ice was beginning to grow along the shoreline. A dozen species of larvae buried themselves for the winter. By January, the surface of the river would freeze all the way across, the ice shelf buried in feet of snow. It was time to drift downstream. Down past the memory of hooks and osprey. Down past the memory of a boy at Benson's Meadow. Down past memories of drifting dories and their floating flies. Down past Farley's Pool and the logjam. Down into the great deep reservoir and deep into Trygve's dreams.

8

The Fisherman's Story
(Tryg, age 10)

I hear and behold God in every object, yet understand god not in the least.

Walt Whitman
Song of Myself

It was dawn, June 20. Even with my warm clothes, gloves and wool cap, I was chilled. Heavy damp fog clung to the river. Father was maybe a hundred yards upstream, my older brother Nicholas downstream. Both had disappeared, swallowed into the mist, as they moved away from me. Three fishermen, waiting in the cold fog on the bank of the Madison River. My first time on the Madison. As the first rays of sun peeked over the fogbank, the gray cloud above me now glowed an iridescent orange.

Inch by inch, the orange blanket began to lift, and the river came into view, calm deep waters, the banks lined with dew-covered grasses up to my waist. My jeans were already soaked from walking across the meadow. With a bit of luck, we three would have this stretch of river, Benson's Meadow, to ourselves. Benson owned this Black Angus grazing land, six miles of calm waters snaking through rich grassland. Fishing by invitation only.

I was just a boy turning eight in September, ready to start fifth grade. The previous summer I had practiced the art of fly fishing for hours with my treasured seven-foot bamboo rod. I was acutely aware of my novice status and intimidated by brother Nicholas, who was already acknowledged by my father's peers as master of rod and reel. His style: meticulous, yet graceful, a strange kind of stern beauty. Nicholas was obsessed by a desire for perfection. He excelled at mechanical drawings and built model three-masted ships, challenged by intricate rigging. He already had a growing business selling his impeccable hand-tied flies.

My father should also have been intimidating. At six foot five, he handled his nine-foot Orvis rod, like a maestro with a wand. But his jovial nature rendered him accessible. When Nicholas fished, his face loomed grim with competitive concentration. I never heard my brother utter a sound when fishing. Father, by contrast, couldn't seem to avoid hooting and laughing whenever he set the hook. Yet, despite their differences, whenever either man cast a fly line, I could almost hear angels singing.

I was awkward and clumsy, determined, but lacking my brother's obsessive zeal. I tried and tried to float a fly into 'that exact spot,' just above a promising pool. Father and Nicholas could effortlessly drop a fly, behind a feathery soft line within a couple inches of a target. Me? Better give me a couple of feet in any direction, the line slapping the water with annoying frequency. I no longer aspire to mastery. I still use my undersized pole--it was my grandfather's and I just love it. I still use a six-pound leader. When I go fishing, I often spend more time watching a muskrat or following an unfamiliar butterfly. My father says, unable to conceal his trademark silly grin, that I'm not a member of "the religion." Nicholas simply expresses contempt: "You must have been adopted," he growls. "No Lindstrom could be so incompetent."

Nicholas was supremely ready for this day. He had a single goal: to catch a trout bigger than the 18-pound rainbow mounted above our fireplace at the cabin. Father had caught the monster two years earlier at his favorite spot where the Fisher River joins the Kootenai a few miles above Libby. It's a place where a lucky angler still might catch a white sturgeon. 18 pounds! Mounted with wide open jaws. I could just fit a baseball among the teeth. An 18-pound rainbow doesn't come close to the Kootenai record 33-pounder, but the biggest trout I'd ever caught so far weighed five pounds, way too small for a taxidermist. This was my brother's chance to catch something really big, to be the Lindstrom champion, using one of his personally created dry flies! I asked father why he didn't display his fish at the office, where patients could admire something other than the terrible artwork. He never answered that question. I'm guessing he felt diffident about showing off. Or maybe a dead fish in a doctor's office is a negative metaphor.

The fog had now lifted perhaps twenty feet above the river, the top layer still glowing orange, the bottom layer now an almost blinding bright white. I wish I had a painter's skill. Gradually the fog simply melted away and the three of us were bathed in the warming rays of early morning. My father and brother each sat in the deep, lush grass near the riverbank. I could now see their heads and shoulders. I sat down too, wondering what was going to happen. Shouldn't we be fishing? I checked my salmon fly, firmly knotted to my six-pound leader. I was glad Nicholas had tied the knot for me, knowing it would hold fast. He insisted on using two-pound test, challenging himself to land big trout on the lightest weight leader.

The rising sun provided glorious, welcome warmth as the dew disappeared on the grass. Then it happened. Hundreds and hundreds of strange larvae began climbing up the grass near the riverbanks. I moved closer to watch. Sometimes two or three of the brown creatures climbed the same stalk of grass which bent under the weight. Every few blades of grass held one or two larvae. Then they stopped moving, resting in the warming sun. I sat just inches from the creatures, as more and more crawled out of the water onto the bank and up stalks of grass. As I watched, the wide thorax of one of the creatures, an inch and a half long, began to split open. What was happening? The body of the creature was tearing apart! Something soft and white and amorphous was trying to ooze out of the torn skin! It was terrible and wonderful all at the same time. In a few minutes a slender insect had crawled out of the brown shell. Then another wondrous thing began! Two wings began unfolding, brown lacy wings, sparkling with dampness, unrolled from the thorax down the long abdomen. At that moment I knew I wanted to become an entomologist. What could possibly be more mysterious, more exciting? I was watching creation! Watching shapeless white flesh transforming into a bright orange abdomen.

The larva spend three or sometimes four years in the water. The great hatches take place sometime between late May and early July. The water temperature needs to be about 55 degrees Fahrenheit, give or take perhaps only one degree.

I watched in complete fascination as more and more skins tore asunder, more and more soft-bodied creatures wriggled out of their shells, magically sprouting legs and a face with large eyes, damp wings unfolding and drying in the sun. One by one, they took to the air, flying awkwardly, disappearing above the meadow and into the pines. Where were they going? Father and Nicholas were still sitting. Why weren't we fishing? At that moment, I could happily have abandoned my bamboo pole to commune with the salmon flies.

Then a terrible thing happened. Wasps! Inch-long yellow and black striped demons. One landed on one of my mysterious creatures as it was just emerging. Then a second and a third wasp joined the assault. They were biting my fly, taking a mouthful of the poor insect and then flying away. Predatory wasps feed flesh to their grubs in paper cells. I was glad my father and Nicholas were too far away to see me. I wept. Although it was but a single insect, the brutality and the suffering unnerved me. Thousands and thousands of bright orange flies were now rising into the air, unharmed, disappearing. Still, I struggled to deal with the jarring juxtaposition of beauty and wickedness, joy and horror.

I felt as if I could barely contain my overflowing cup of emotions. I was just a boy, invited to fish on what felt like hallowed ground. Waiting impatiently to fish, I had become immersed in wondrous spectacle after spectacle: the glowing fog, metamorphosis, the predation of wasps.

What happened next will be carved into my memory until my final day. The salmon flies were returning, swirling like a black tornado. They floated over the pines in an ominous black cloud, blotting the sun and casting a dark shadow over Benson's Meadow. They began descending on the river. The entire surface, so recently hidden by fog, now disappeared again under millions of salmon flies, skimming the river, mating and dropping eggs. Then the roar! Like a sudden waterfall. The fish! Thousands of fish! Leaping and splashing and gulping mouthfuls of flies. I heard my father shout, "Time to fish, boy! Time to fish!" followed by his unmistakable roar of laughter. I had nearly forgotten about fishing! I unhooked my salmon fly from the pole's eyelet. The river seemed to be boiling. Trembling, I managed to cast into a chaotic turbulence of swarming flies and leaping fish.

First cast: I felt the electric jolt. I had a fish! Something really big! My reel was spinning as the fish raced downstream. There's no drag on a fly reel, but I pressed my thumb on the line, feeling the warmth of friction as yard after yard of line raced downstream. My rod bounced crazily, bending nearly in half. It was a light pole, decades old. and I was afraid it might break. I quickly glanced upstream, hoping Father was watching. Then I heard him hollering, "Hooray, boy!" he called. I hoped he might join me, help me net the fish, give me some fatherly advice, but he was busy with his own dancing pole. Yet I felt a sudden surge of pride; I was fishing on my own.

Suddenly the line went slack. Oh no! I've lost it. I didn't care so much about the fish as the inevitable critique my brother would certainly deliver. I reeled in my line as quickly as I could and then felt the jolt! I nearly lost the pole as it jerked, bending in half, the line again flying from the reel. The fish had reversed course and was now charging upstream against the current. Oh, the sheer excitement, the heart-pounding thrill! I wanted to holler like Dad, but I could barely breathe with excitement. I trotted along the bank, up and down the river, trying to keep up with my opponent. Three times the fish dove deep into a pool and then leapt into the air in a fountain of spray, crashing back into the river with a loud thump.

Sometimes I reeled frantically, recovering the bright yellow line whenever the fish changed directions only to feel another burst of speed, and I'd lose all the line I had just gained. I no longer had the energy to race along the bank; I let the fish race and turn and race again, dive and leap and dive again. Gradually I sensed I was making progress. The dashes up and downriver became shorter; the fishline began accumulating on the reel. Time seemed to stop. I must have struggled for at least half an hour, perhaps twice that long. The air was filled with swarming salmon flies and diving swallows. The water roiled with the madness of feeding trout. My rod danced to a mighty fish struggle, my heart pounding with sensory overload as I alternately reeled in line and felt the fish pull away in yet another heroic run. Then the fish came into view. It actually scared me. It must have been a yard long and nearly a foot deep from dorsal to ventral fin. Oh, so carefully did I tug the fish closer and closer. The monster had finally surrendered. I waded into the shallows. The great beast was done in. It lay on its side: I could see an array of bright red circles shining in the sun along its massive body. It was a brown trout.

I should have tried my net, but the fish was a foot longer than my landing net. I reached near the mouth of the fish and lifted it up by the leader. Oh, the heartbreak. The stupidity. I should have buried my hand in the gills. There was still plenty of life in the creature as it whipped back and forth, snapping the leader, dropping into the water, disappearing in a flash. It was years later that Father confessed to stifling his laughter when he saw my trophy escape. I'm sure that Nicholas forever holds me in unmitigated contempt for my failure. Nicholas called the day a "disappointment." Although he caught dozens of trout, he failed to land a challenge to Father's mounted fish.

I caught rainbows and even a grayling, releasing each one carefully, admiring their beauty. I'm glad that huge brown trout escaped. If I had landed it, I would have killed it. Father would have taken it to a taxidermist. It would be hanging on a wall somewhere. But not on my wall. I could never look at it without sadness.

Godspeed, my beauty.

9

A Tale of Two Books
(Tryg, age 10)

Knowledge puffs up, but love edifies.

1 Corinthians 8:1

I do not laugh;
(I'm Norwegian;
We frown on laughter
In the polar region).

I do not chuckle;
I seldom smile.
My face is neutral
As bathroom tile.

I do not titter;
Conceal my passion.
To Norwegians, emotion
Is out of fashion.

Girls, blink your lashes;
Expose black silk.
I'll watch, unmoved,
As a mug of milk.

When I talk to a girl,
I stare at my shoes.
I don't play games,
So, I never lose.

We Norskies have a reputation
Slow-witted, hardy, sometimes daring.
We consider gourmet fare
A smorgasbord of pickled herring.

I'm rather shy and introverted,
Won't find me wearing colorful tights.
But even I can't refrain from weeping
When I watch the northern lights.

Tryg Lindstrom
"My Brother Nicholas, a True Norwegian"
From *Poems for Posterity*

It's not easy being an entomologist with limited financial resources. Tryg's list of "necessities" seemed never-ending. With the help of the librarian, Tryg wrote a company in Brooklyn called The Butterfly Company. They sent a catalog with butterflies, moths and beetles for sale, insect pins, balsa wood spreading boards, Riker mounts, relaxing fluid. But the cost! As usual, Tryg marshalled his arguments carefully. Supplies could be considered part of his education. Conrad, always a pushover, said he'd give Tryg $50; after all, he'd given Nicholas nearly two hundred dollars for a special mathematical calculator. Fifty dollars! It was far more than he had expected. Tryg spent days deciding what to buy. He chose packets of 100 Elephant brand "professional, black-coated steel insect pins" in five different sizes, two spreading boards, a dozen Riker mounts in various sizes (not nearly as good or professional as insect cases, but affordable and far superior to his cigar boxes), and the rest of his funds he spent on butterflies and moths. The problem with ordering insects was that Tryg had no idea what he was buying. He had to rely on the catalog descriptions. He wished for pictures, especially in color. Some specimens were labelled A-2 or B ("minor flaws" or "damaged"). Tryg made sure he selected only A-1, "perfect or ex pupae." Nowhere could he find pictures of butterflies or moths listed in the South America or Africa section. He assumed the expensive insects must be the most spectacular.

He chose two "birdwing gems" - butterflies from Africa, a pair of giant moon moths and "the gloriously iridescent dayflying moth" from Madagascar, the "spectacular blue and black" Ulysses swallowtail from the Solomon Islands and "BEST VALUE showy collection of twenty different worldwide butterflies." Alas, his small fortune, the entire 50 dollars was spent, with 11 cents left over after paying for postage.

Tryg's next challenge was finding a place to work. The bedroom was too small. He needed a desk. He needed his own laboratory. The basement! The old house had a full basement. The old wood-burning furnace and a large supply of Pres-to-Logs sat at the bottom of the stairs. Then there was Mother's small laundry with washer, dryer and a large sink that no one ever used. Behind the stairs was a large room with the ping pong table, where Nicholas, Conrad and Tryg had battled for hours, Tryg slowly learning to play a competitive game. Behind that room, the knotty pine guest bedroom with its own bathroom. And finally, in the far corner was a small room with Mother's compact oak roll-top desk. Mother loved her little desk with convenient drawers and cubby holes. It was where she paid the bills and wrote Christmas cards. But she had allowed Nicholas to tie his exquisite flies at that desk as long as he removed his feathers and paraphernalia at the end of the day. No worries there. Nicholas always left his mother's desk exactly as he had found it.

But Tryg was notoriously unreliable in keeping things neat and tidy. How could he convince Mother that he'd create his "laboratory" for a few hours and then return Mother's desk to her in its original condition as Nicholas had done. Tryg knew he'd have to make solemn promises. Anna, admittedly a bit reluctant, said she'd give it a try. Tryg was in business! A week passed. No package from Brooklyn. Another week passed. Conrad's check had cleared the bank, but each day the postman's delivery was a disappointment. After school the next week, Tryg raced home on his bike and burst into the living room. Oh joy! Two large boxes sat on the coffee table addressed to "Master Trygve Lindstrom."

He tore open the heaviest box first. Riker mounts! They ranged in size from 12 x 16 inches to two small 3 x 4 ones. Tryg admired the cardboard frames wrapped in black paper, the soft cotton batting and the glass fronts. On the back of the mounts were hangers on the short and long side. Tyrg pulled out two balsa spreading boards and five packets of "Elephant Insect Pins: The World's Finest."

The other box was large, but much lighter in weight. His butterflies! In several places on the outside of the carton a red stamp shouted "Fragile." Anna had joined Tryg in his breathless excitement. She thought about insisting that Tryg wait until Conrad came home but didn't have the heart to make her son wait. Tryg secured a sharp knife and carefully cut the tape. Then, with unaccustomed caution, he lifted out four boxes. The first box was a foot long and eight inches wide. He carefully lifted off the cover and then the layer of cotton batting to reveal two large paper triangles. He lifted the top triangle--oh the wonder of it! Inside, barely visible, he made out the outline of a huge moth with long tails. The body alone was nearly five centimeters long. The envelope read "*Argema mittrei*, male, ex pupa, Antanarivo, Malagassy Republic." It's a moon moth, Mother," he blurted. "I have my very own moon moth! Let me show you a picture." Tryg ran to the *National Geographic* magazine article entitled, "Madagascar: Land of Wonders" and showed the color photograph of the wonderful creature.

"I'm going to save these for last," he announced. "I need to practice on less valuable specimens." He opened each box with excited reverence, slowly reading each name: *Urania riphaeus, Papilio ulysses, Ornithoptera antimachus, Ornithoptera zalmoxis*. He said the names over and over, celebrated them, absorbed them. What pleasure he experienced each time he spoke the words. He decided to start with his "BEST VALUE" collection of 20 assorted worldwide butterflies.

Tryg was well prepared. He started with six small envelopes. He knew how to steam them overnight. He brought his six envelopes down to the basement, placed the spreading boards, pins, paper strips. The next morning, he unwrapped the first envelope ever so carefully, delighted to see the swirls of red and black on white hindwings. He pinched the thorax, please to see the wings unfold. The insect was perfectly "relaxed." While still pinching he selected one of the smallest pins and eased it through the center of the thorax and pinned the specimen in the center groove of the spreading board. Now came the tricky part: spreading the wings, adjusting them exactly as he wanted them displayed and then securing the wings under his paper strips. Disaster!

As he lowered the wings on the left, the entire insect twisted out of the groove. The paper strips rubbed off wing scales. As he carefully moved a wing with a pin, he left a small hole. Then, securing the antennae, he broke one off. He tried using glass microscope slides to hold down the wings, but scales hung to the glass. He tried adjusting wings with his stamp tongs, better. The delicate tiny tails of an especially beautiful blue and green butterfly (*Thecla coronata*) fell off when he removed the paper strips. The first butterfly, so beautifully marked on the underside was unremarkable, so he placed it in the Riker mount upside down. When he gently lowered the glass top, all four wings broke. Six pinned butterflies, six disappointments.

Tryg cleaned the desktop, taking his equipment upstairs to his room. He made sure that everything was Nicholas-clean before lowering the roll top. But he was disheartened. At least his efforts had been exerted on the least expensive butterflies. He decided that the next day he'd try again, with six more guinea pigs. But would he dare to try his hand on a moon moth or *Ornithoptera zalmoxis*?

That night, after his father returned from rounds and settled into his chair, Tryg asked if he could talk. Conrad put down his medical journal. He recognized the signs. Tryg had something important to say.

"Father," he began. Here are two books, *The Moth Book* by Holland

and *The Spider Book* by Comstock. I can hardly read *The Spider Book*. It's more than 700 pages long. Let me read a sentence to you." He opened the book to a random page and read, "The Tetragnathinae agree with the Metinae in the absence of transverse furrows on the epigastric plates; but can be distinguished from them by the fact that the epigastric furrow between the spiracles is procurved."

Conrad started to chuckle, then erupted into a roar of laughter. Tryg was about to become angry with his father and then began laughing as well. When they both regained their composure, Tryg continued. "That was page 406. Just about any page is just as bad. The librarian says it's the most definitive spider book ever written. But who could ever read a book like this?"

Conrad suppressed another outburst of laughter.

Tryg continued. "Holland's book is filled with technical stuff. He illustrates each moth's specific wing venation. Who cares about wing venation! He mentions anatomical details. But look at this." Tryg showed color plate after color plate of moths. "Look at these wonderful pictures. The majority of these thousands of moths, Holland caught and mounted himself and donated to the Carnegie Museum. But this book has treasures. Besides all the technical stuff, Holland talks about making a concoction of stale beer and rum and sugar and going out at night to paint trees with the stuff. Now listen to this: 'In our pockets are our cyanide jars. . . . Let us stealthily approach the next tree. . . . What is there? Oho! My beauty!'"

"Listen to this paragraph," Tryg continued. "'When the hour of dark approaches stand by a bed of evening primroses, and as their great yellow blossoms suddenly open, watch the hawkmoths coming as swiftly as meteors through the air, hovering for an instant over this blossom, probing into the sweet depths of another, and then dashing off again so quickly that the eye cannot follow them.'"

"Here's how Holland ends his book: 'When the moon shall have faded out from the sky, and the sun shall shine at noonday a dull cherry-red, and the seas shall be frozen over, and the ice-cap shall have crept downward to the equator from either pole, and no keels shall cut the waters, nor wheels turn in mills, when all cities hall have long been dead and crumbled into dust, and all life shall be on the very verge of extinction on this globe; then, on one bit of lichen, growing on the bald rocks beside the eternal snows . . . shall be seated a tiny insect, preening its antenna in the glow of the worn-out sun.'"

"Two books," Tryg said, getting to his point. "One reminds me of Nicholas--technical, precise, but, well, without *something!* Without emotion. Without . . . without *joy*. Holland is filled with joy. He *loves* what he's doing. He's excited.

"It's the same with the lovely insects I just got. They need someone like Nicholas to set them perfectly. They need someone who can tie a perfect dry fly. I'm not a--I'm not a *technician*. I don't want to spend thousands of hours creating perfect specimens where every feather on a moth's feathered antennae is perfect. I want someone else to do that kind of work. Oh yes, I want a moon moth on my wall, a perfect one, and the beautiful butterflies I bought. I want to show them to people. I want them displayed on my wall. And Father . . . I feel kind of guilty about wasting your money on those Riker mounts. They're just, they're just not what I need."

"Son," Conrad said, "when I was a young boy, I knew I wanted to be a doctor. More than *wanted* . . . I *had* to be a doctor. In some strange way, I thought I already was a doctor. I just needed time and study and diplomas and residency and so much to learn to make it official. You *know* you're an entomologist. And you even know what kind of entomologist you're going to be and not going to be. Anna and I have seen how happy you are whenever you find a click beetle. Wasps . . . not so much." He tried to stop himself but started laughing; Tryg looked down in embarrassment and then joined his father. "But it took me a long time to discover what I was not. I'm not a big city doctor. I need to live by rivers and lakes. I need to raise my sons in a small town. Anna needed to escape mosquitoes. Those paint by numbers paintings in my office . . . they're pretty awful. But you know what? I love them, every one of them. Even the one that's kind of the town joke with random splatters of paint. I'm a country doctor. At Christmas we get jerky and huckleberry jam and Bertha Mae tells me how much money I should have gotten. But this is where I belong. This is who I am.

You're starting to learn where you belong. Return *The Spider Book* to the library. Somebody's probably going to write a spider book you will love. Maybe it's already been written. He, or she, may talk about those epigastric plates, but also the drama of spiders capturing prey or how the female eats the male after mating or about keeping a tarantula as a pet and watching it shed its skin. Let's give the Riker mounts to your science teacher. And let's see if you can convince Nicholas to do his magic with your moon moths. I'll get Mr. Sjernholm to make a few proper display boxes for your special insects. He's a cabinet builder, so I know he'll build exactly what you need. Besides, he owes me for his gallbladder surgery."

Conrad stopped speaking. Tryg was silent. Both had spoken; both felt comfortable in the moment.

Anna called from the kitchen, "Huck pie and ice cream!"

10

The Cricket Hunter
(Tryg, age 11)

One day, on tearing of some old bark, I saw two rare beetles, and seized one in each hand; then I saw a third and new kind, which I would not bear to lose, so that I popped the one which I held in my right hand into my mouth. Alas! It ejected some intensely acrid fluid, which burnt my tongue so that I was forced to spit the beetle out, which was lost, as was the third one.

Charles Darwin
The Life and Letters of Charles Darwin

Tryg spent nearly half of summer vacation at the cabin with his mother. His father joined them Friday evenings, making the 55-mile drive from Libby after seeing the final patient of the day. Sherlock, the family basset, enjoyed sitting in the front seat of Conrad's Jeep, ears flapping in the breeze of the open window. Early Sunday morning the three (and Sherlock) returned to Libby. Anna played the little pump organ at the small Episcopal church and insisted on her "three boys" filling one of the small pews.

Nicholas usually stayed in town, earning money at the drug store for college. Tryg was glad for the distance separating them, avoiding the stress of competing with his older brother. Tryg loved his summers. Once in a while one of his friends would join him for a few days. But

Tryg preferred his independence. His friends showed little interest in collecting bugs. They preferred cruising in the small motorboat and fishing, swimming and shooting their .22 rifles. Otto was Tryg's most frequent visitor. On his last visit, Otto had been eager to go across the lake to see the eagle nest, but when they arrived, he produced his father's pipe filled with tobacco. "I kind of borrowed it," Otto admitted sheepishly. "Dad will never notice the pipe's missing; he has about a dozen of 'em." Otto tried a few puffs first; the "Dutch Treat" tobacco smelled pleasant enough. Then Tryg took his turn, grimacing at the bitter taste of nicotine. He returned the pipe to Otto, who gamely puffed on the pipe as the boat rocked to the gentle waves. Suddenly he turned ashen, leaned over the side of the boat and threw up. On the way back to the cabin, Otto sat in the bow, gulping fresh air and moaning.

When not burdened with entertaining classmates, Tryg often zoomed across the lake in the family's 12-foot red fiberglass boat, powered by a 10 horsepower Evenrude outboard, to that bald eagle nest. "Zoomed" was perhaps hyperbolic; the boat was probably the smallest on the lake with the smallest outboard motor, but satisfyingly speedy for a boy of eight. Every year the eagles returned to the tallest tamarack on the opposite shore, adding sticks to the nest and raising two or three or even four chicks. He'd drift near the shore, drop anchor, and delight to the loud "peep, peep" of hungry chicks. Soon one of the adults would arrive with a fish. He watched and listened, perfectly content.

Another favorite activity was snagging suckers that came near the shore every spring, lured by the roe of the mating silver salmon. He was never able to entice the "trash fish" to take a fly or lure or bait, but he had learned to snag them occasionally with a large treble-hooked spoon. With his father's spinning rod he'd cast into deep water and then drag the spoon slowly over the rocky lake bottom where hundreds of bright red spawning suckers gathered. Each caught sucker ended up buried in Conrad's raspberry patch as fertilizer. Anna's favorite breakfast was a bowl of raspberries in cream and brown sugar. Keep Anna happy and a dozen of the world's best cinnamon rolls might fill the kitchen with an aroma of yeast and cinnamon.

Tryg often climbed the hill across Highway 2, where he might spot a porcupine or bobcat or black bear. Bears were frequent visitors to the dump. It was his favorite place to target practice with his single-shot Marlin .22 rifle, a prized eighth year birthday present. Once Tryg had shot a squirrel trapped high in a tree. It fell at his feet, lifeless eyes staring at him accusingly. He'd be haunted for the rest of his life by the memory. He never was able to tell his parents of his cowardly act.

One particularly memorable August day picking huckleberries at his secret spot, (Montanans jealousy guard their favorite fishing hole and their secluded huckleberry patch) he spied two adorable bear cubs 50 yards to his right. Instantly alert, Tryg then saw the mother loping down the hill toward him on his left. Tryg fired a shot into the air, hoping to frighten the bears. The cubs raced to the mother. Tryg didn't wait to find out what the mother bear was doing as he quickly retreated home; another story he kept to himself.

Summer days often found Tryg lying on the edge of the dock, waiting for hellgrammites to crawl out of the water, up the posts and then metamorphose into dragonflies. He now had more than a dozen pristine specimens, his pride being a one with a bright red body. Dragonflies were one of his "expensive" insects. He could barely fit five or six in a cigar box. One cigar box cost him a quarter, or 75 cents if it was a prized wooden box. He reserved his wooden boxes for the showiest specimens. He only had three wooden boxes so far, so he saved them for his largest finds. One of the wooden boxes had a black ground beetle, a metallic beetle, a spectacular 7cm ichneumon wasp, two salmon flies and a robber fly. He reserved the final spot for a "thumb cricket," One unexpected benefit of storing insects in cigar boxes: the tobacco residue seemed to discourage museum beetles, tiny insects that devoured specimens, turning them to dust. He had six sphynx moths in one wooden box; two black swallowtails in another, and a mated pair of cecropia moths waiting to be transferred to the next wooden box.

He especially liked large insects, avoiding specimens the size of ladybugs or smaller. Tryg spent countless hours watching and collecting insects. He had become skilled at knowing where to hunt. Yellow longhorn beetles favored goldenrod blossoms. In the spring, he'd watch for the large queen bumblebees that visited his father's foxgloves. Lovely green sweat bees favored lupine but were too small to collect. The best insect hunting was at night, the cabin's back porchlight attracting a wonderful variety, particularly moths.

At 10:30 p.m. the diminishing tangerine dusky glow still lingered above the lakeshore. Water skiers and fishermen had pulled their boats out of the water. The last logging truck had long since rumbled down Boisvert's Hill toward Libby's lumber mill, some 55 miles west. Except for the distant whoosh of an occasional car on U.S. Highway 2, human sounds had given way to gentle lapping of ripples, splashing fish and the occasional forlorn coyote's lament. The last darting swallows now deferred to acrobatic bats skimming the surface of the lake. Rainbows and silver salmon fed hungrily on newly hatched mayflies.

Inside the one-bedroom log cabin, the Lindstroms settled down to their accustomed subdued Friday evening. Anna sat on her embroidered platform rocker, in front of the crackling log fire, working her way through the Sunday *New York Times* crossword puzzle with a ballpoint pen. I heard The Trout Quintet on the record player. Tryg and his father indulged Anna's preferences for Cole, Harry Belafonte, and Bing Crosby. At least they didn't have to listen to Frank Sinatra, Tryg thought with a shudder. The turntable held only one record at a time. Anna and Conrad alternated their choices; the next well-used vinyl disc might be Vivaldi, Bach, Handel, Tchaikovsky, Grieg, Tom Lehrer or *The Sound of Music*. Most Saturday evenings the elder Lindstroms spent an hour or more providing their own live music, Conrad gamely bowing his beloved cello while Anna contributed a far more accomplished violin.

Conrad nestled in his deep-green, well-worn tufted leather armchair, slippered feet resting on the matching ottoman, reading one of the recently delivered medical journals and sipping The Balvenie, his favorite single-malt whisky. He had just finished a favorite late-night snack: a bowl of crushed saltine crackers in buttermilk. Everyone in Libby knew his office hours ended at 2 p.m. on Friday, nurses heading home at 3 ("come hell or high water," Bertha Mae often announced) even if the waiting room still had patients. As usual "Doc" had stayed for the stragglers and apologetic walk-ins, some who had no money and didn't want to be scolded by the formidable Bertha Mae. Behind her back, far behind her back, patients called her "Big Bertha," or "Battle Axe Bertha," or simply "That Woman." Don't even *think* about bringing a dog into the office when Bertha Mae was on duty. Conrad didn't mind dogs in the office but couldn't risk losing a nurse over the issue. And you had better fill out every line on the new-patient form or face That Woman's frown, fists placed on her substantial hips.

Nurse Bertha also did her best to collect payments from patients before they left the office. Families from the mine and the mill had good insurance and typically paid at least the $5 office visit co-pay. Other charges generally waited for the insurance company to negotiate. But most of the shopkeepers and self-employed had no health insurance. Bertha Mae insisted they pay at least a portion of any bill and then promptly sent an invoice for the balance. Thirty days later, she'd send a second notice. Every time she sent a second notice she scolded "Doctor," whose policy was to ignore any debts after the second invoice. Bertha Mae fumed, fussed and ranted to Doctor's deaf ears. By the same token, his intrepid nurse refused to listen to Conrad's arguments:

> *These people are our friends and neighbors.*
> *Some of these folks struggle to buy food and firewood.*
> *We're not going to start legal actions against our patients.*
> *I get paid in venison and artwork and huckleberry jam.*
> *Sometimes patients come in months later and surprise us with a payment.*
> *Some folks might stop seeking our help if they worry about past-due bills.*

Bertha Mae knew she'd never win. But she *knew* she was right. Even though Doc Conrad ignored delinquent payments, Bertha Mae kept all the records. At the end of each year, she'd add up all the money owed (subtracting a generous 25 percent for "venison, "works of art," pickled whitefish and other sundries." Last year, she noted, Doctor had chosen to ignore the princely sum of $3,200 in uncollected fees.

Conrad's other nurse, Jennie, was older and considerably more mellow, than her colleague. Perhaps Bertha Mae had used up all the irritability and impatience in the room. Jennie refused to have any part of the billing and left as much of the filing as she could to Bertha Mae. Bertha Mae took special pride in her well-kept files and preferred that Jennie focus on the patients. Jennie was a gifted phlebotomist, particularly adept with older patients, and a gem at making children comfortable. She had supervised the decoration of one of Conrad's three small patient rooms especially for kids (the giraffe on the wall marked with feet and inches) with bright colors and a bin filled with stuffed animals and assorted toys. Bertha Mae thought the room was a waste of time and money. Whenever it was time for children's inoculations, Nurse Jennie often came to Conrad's rescue, the doctor not wanting kids to associate him with pain.

But now the Lindstrom family was together for another summer weekend. Conrad held his bent pipe between his teeth, puffing contentedly on an unlit bowl of fresh tobacco. Later he'd walk out to the end of their dock and smoke the sweet vanilla-flavored Fjord, ordered once a month from his tobacconist in Minneapolis. Anna studiously ignored Conrad's most salient vices - his taste for single malt whiskies and pipe tobacco, but she put her foot down firmly: no smoking inside the cabin or in their Libby home. Conrad skipped over the article "Anomalies of the Gall Bladder," bearing his name. "Doc Conrad," as pretty much everyone in Libby called him, was something of an anomaly himself, a country doctor who made house calls and a board-certified vascular surgeon with published articles in the likes of *The New England Journal of Medicine* and the *Journal of the American Medical Association*.

Tryg began gathering his collecting jars and flashlight. "B O B," Tryg called out cheerfully.

"OK," his mother responded, chuckling as she always did when her precocious and quirky son used one of his pet acronyms. "B O B" meant "be out back." "Misiball meant "may I stay in bed a little longer?" (He hated getting up before nine on weekends and during the summer). "WAPForP" was Anna's current favorite: "writing a poem for posterity." Tryg had confidently entitled his journals (already burgeoning to volume three) *Poems for Posterity*. His latest, set to music, (he was making progress on his baritone ukelele) still awaited a title:

I don't know much, but this I know:
That deer leave footprints in the snow
That evening follows every day;
That children laugh and play.

I don't hear much, but this I hear:
The pine trees whisper joy and fear,
A tired man sit down and sigh,
A tiny baby cry.

I don't see much. But this I see:
An eagle's nest high in a tree,
A boy and girl walk hand and hand,
A seashell on the sand.

Occasionally, Tryg looked at his earliest poems, embarrassed by his efforts. Anna insisted that he keep them, saying that his journals were precious. She was certain that poet laureates typically kept their juvenalia. Tryg agreed to indulge his mother's, well, "mothering." But what terrible poems he had written!

I love the Lord and he loves me.
I know that I will never be

As kind and good as He will be.
'Cause he's the Lord and I'm just me.

He felt queasy reading the first poem in his first journal. Maybe one day he'd accidentally drop that journal into the trash. He hoped no one would ever read:

An eagle fought a seagull.
A hunter shot his gun.
Missed the seagull, hit the eagle.
So the seagull won.

He shut the small journal, embarrassed. Time to go cricket hunting.

Tryg walked out to the back porch and looked carefully. The back wall of the cabin, lit by two outside lights, was spotted with insects. He ignored mosquitoes whining past his ears, and scarcely noticed pedestrian miller moths and crane flies. He scanned the wall with a discerning eye. Aha! A prize, a fine brown longhorn beetle nearly five centimeters long. (He now insisted on converting every scientific measurement into the "proper" metric system.) Tryg put his collecting gear on the outside porch wood box and moved closer to his prey. He was already familiar with its habits. The beetle would stay motionless, scarcely budging even when brushed by an errant moth. What was it doing? Tryg hadn't figured that out yet.

Smaller longhorns fed and mated on wildflowers during the day (making it easy for him to put "male" and "female" symbols in his journal), but this occasional visitor just *rested* on the cabin wall, sometimes for hours, and then left by morning's light. Must be waiting for a mate, Tryg speculated. He stood directly behind the beetle, deftly pressing his index finger over the beetle's elytra and then pinching its thorax. Ouch! The beetle had a sharp thorn-shaped spike on either side of its thorax, puncturing Tryg's thumb and forefinger. Still, he refused to let go of his prize. The beetle waved its legs in protest, sharp mandibles futilely pinching the air. He marveled at the power in the struggling legs and knew firsthand how those jaws could bite into skin. It was his second specimen, but he couldn't resist another example of the largest beetle he'd ever seen alive. If only Montana had the giants of the tropics. Oh, to see the 15 cm *Titaneus giganteus* or the gigantic moon moth of Madagascar, (both featured in a favorite copy of *National Geographic*).

Tryg unscrewed the lid of a wide-mouth glass jar and dropped in his trophy. The beetle made a couple of desultory circuits around the base of the jar, sliding on the glass, and then settled down. Tryg looked at the two puncture wounds. At least there seemed to be no irritant or toxin. He wondered if some longhorn beetles armed with similar spikes could inflict toxins. Some caterpillars emitted poison from their spiked bodies. Certain ground beetles sprayed hot ammonia and he had read about a millipede in the tropics that squirted cyanide. He vowed to learn more.

Within a few minutes, he had collected two owlet moths (separate jar) and a robber fly (an unusual find at night)—already a pretty good night's work. He saw a beautiful 10-centimeter *cecropia* moth, identifying it as a male by its wide bipectinated antennae. (It felt so good to use words like "bipectinated.") But he already had a mated pair of specimens, (*ex-pupae* he had proudly added to the descriptive label) and saw no reason to collect another, especially a large moth that would take up so much space in his limited supply of cigar boxes.

He had actually heard the female *cecropia* scratching her way out of the brown leathery cocoon and had offered his index finger as a resting place for her to complete the ineffable mystery of metamorphosis. Half an hour later the perfect specimen sprayed his t-shirt with a viscous yellow liquid—Tryg's signal to dispatch the specimen with a sharp pinch of thumb and forefinger to her thorax. Tryg berated himself for his unscientific reluctance to kill. He had already grown attached to the trusting moth. Now she was just another artistically displayed and labeled specimen, *Samia cecropia*. He had even gone to the trouble of displaying two empty cocoons, one sliced open to show its smooth woody interior.

He wanted to show others the wonders of his discoveries, to share his excitement, to appreciate the beauty, the drama and even the cruelty of insects.

Tryg took his flashlight and the remaining collecting jar, entered the adjacent woods and turned his attention to trickier quarry. The rhythmic chirping of crickets alternated from bush to bush. Tryg walked as silently and slowly as possible toward the nearest sound. His well-practiced hunt was painstakingly slow. Whenever he began to zero in on a sound, the wary nearby insect grew silent; Tryg froze in place, hoping the cricket would again respond to the intermittent chirping that echoed throughout the woods. It was almost as if they were teasing him, chirping until he got too close, and then trying to lure him to a more distant sound. Tryg's journals recorded dozens of "cricket safaris" ending without even a glimpse of his prey. This time Tryg refused to be led astray by the siren voices of others. He knew he was close. Tryg ignored the nearby great horned owl hooting. He often spotted the bird, two bright orange eyes reflected in his flashlight. But tonight, he refused to be distracted.

"*Chirp*"! So close! Tryg turned his head, pointing his ear to locate the exact position. He was sure he had isolated the right kinnikinnick bush these crickets favored. He waited like a statue, minute after patient minute. Half a dozen crickets chirped intermittently around him, but Tryg stayed immobile. *Chirp!* Tryg refocused on the sound and turned on the flashlight. Centered on the beam of light, he spotted two brown hind legs. These insects conceal themselves underneath the kinnikinnick foliage, usually invisible from above. Silently, methodically, he removed the top of the wide-mouthed jar and positioned it under the bush directly below the exposed hind legs. The fat brown cricket let go of its perch and dropped. Tryg, familiar with the cricket's escape ploy, thrilled to the satisfying "plunk" of specimen falling into the waiting jar. "Gotcha," he whispered in triumph. He took a moment to admire the strange insect he called a "thumb cricket" after the size of the first digit of his father's thumb. The insect was armed with an alarming but harmless sword of an ovipositor and six-centimeter-long antennae as fine as a strand of hair. The conquering hero gathered up his prizes and re-entered the cabin.

"I'm back," he called out, glad for the cabin's warmth.

He heard his parents mumble some vague assent from their bedroom. It was nearly one. He sat down at the dining room table and looked closely at the large cricket, nearly as long as his largest beetle, stocky as a bulldog yet sporting incongruously delicate antennae. He could make a few girls at school scream at the cricket's "stinger," he thought. Too bad it was summer vacation. The fireplace still glowed dimly with orange coals, occasionally spurting a wisp of blue flame. Tryg loved the quiet of the evening and despite the late hour, knew he had more work to do. He rummaged in the closet and brought out a small cardboard cigar box. His older brother, Nicholas, brought home a box or two every month from the drug store, collecting the fee. Tryg laid out his modest equipment—notebook and pen, a tin of straight pins, strips of typing paper, two balsa wood boards. Flicking open the nozzle on the bright yellow can of lighter fluid, he squeezed a few drops into one jar. The two moths succumbed in an instant, legs and wings tightly folded downward, over the body and legs. Tryg worked deliberately.

Tryg held the first moth carefully between the index finger and thumb of his left hand, and then slid the pin through the center of the furry thorax. Down the center of his balsa wood board he had carved a groove, just like the one pictured in his beloved *The Butterfly Book*. Spreading wings was always a challenge. If he used his fingers, tiny bits of scales rubbed off. How did they do it in museums, he wondered? His best tool was stamp tongs. He coveted the six specialized "insect forceps" illustrated in Holland's book, but his tongs worked well. As he began moving the forewing into the position, the moth pivoted on the pin. He started over. This time, he secured the moth in place by inserting pins on either side of its abdomen. Once he had positioned a forewing exactly where he wanted it, he carefully held it down under a thin strip of typing paper, inserting pins through the paper close to the wing. It was harder to spread the lower wings away from the moth's body, but Tryg had acquired considerable dexterity through countless hours of practice and many a heartbreak of torn wings and broken antennae. He felt a thrill of pleasure when the underwings revealed bright yellow and black stripes. Gently he spread the moth to the standard display position. The last step was pinning the antennae and recording the specimen in his notebook on the page with the current date:

unidentified owlet moth
family Noctuidae
McGregor Lake, MT

Tryg now took time to admire his first perfect "thumb cricket." The only other specimen he had managed to catch had a broken antenna, so he had returned her to the woods, instructing her to be fruitful and multiply. Tryg knew he'd have to treat these delicate appendages with special care. The cricket died quickly in the lighter fluid, a killing agent that evaporated in a few seconds and so far that had never ruined the natural color of his specimens. The straight pin was just long enough to penetrate the cricket's thorax and secure its body to the balsa wood spreading board. Using pairs of pins like scissors, he positioned the antennae in symmetrical curves. He was pleased with his work and looked forward to this handsome specimen displayed in her reserved spot. In an ordinary cigar box he displayed his two other cricket species, a pudgy black 2cm one that had hopped clumsily on the ground and a lovely, delicate green one that chirped from trees.

Next: the longhorn beetle. *Cerambycidae,* he mumbled to himself, proud to identify at least the family name. But he was distressed. Lighter fluid just wasn't effective against these beetles. With the moths and cricket, the legs had folded up in death within seconds. This beetle seemed immune to lighter fluid. Tryg knew that "real" entomologists like Holland had killing jars with chloroform and cyanide-soaked plaster of Paris in the base. Parental permissiveness did not extend to Tryg's handling of cyanide, so lighter fluid became the default poison. It didn't work well on most beetles. Suddenly, Tryg felt a familiar wave of frustration. There must be a safe and effective killing agent.

He tried another squirt of fluid. Still nothing. He turned the bottle upside down and the beetle dropped to the table. Despite the beetle's size and impressive mandibles, it was surprisingly passive. Tryg lifted the jar and grabbed the insect at the thorax, this time safely behind the sharp thorns. He then pinned the beetle on the right side through the elytrum, exactly as his *Field Guide to Western Insects* showed. Sometimes, with brightly colored metallic beetles, he took artistic license and spread the elytra and leathery wings to expose a shiny abdomen, displaying the insect in flight, but this giant was drab underneath. Besides, spread wings took up additional valuable storage space.

Tryg felt deeply uncomfortable pinning a live insect, but he didn't know what else to do. If he waited for the hapless insect to die, he risked dealing with a brittle specimen and broken appendages. His small arsenal of alternative poisons had their limitations as well. Paint thinner sometimes bleached a prize insect, and he didn't want to take a chance. His mother's hair spray was terrific, killing spiders and most insects instantly, but the sticky residue was unacceptable. Maybe the pharmacist (with Tryg's father's approval, of course) could suggest something. He carefully pinned the beetle's squirming legs and antennae in position and recorded the capture in his journal. When he had finished his last entry, he placed the balsa wood boards on top of the kitchen pantry, put his modest equipment back in the box and got ready for bed, the living room couch that became a hideaway bed. In the bedroom, Conrad was sitting up, coughing.

Before he went to sleep, Tryg composed and practiced his speech for the morning.

11

Aebleskivers
(Tryg, age 11)

I suppose you are an entomologist?

Not quite as ambitious as that, sir. No man can truly be called an entomologist, sir; the subject is too vast for any single human intelligence to grasp.

Oliver Wendell Holmes
The Poet at the Breakfast Table

As usual during the summer, Tryg was the last to rise in the morning. Alert to the delightful, intermingled aromas of percolating Folger's coffee and Polish sausages boiling in an inch of water in the frying pan, he padded into the kitchen still dressed in blue plaid flannel pajamas. Breakfast was going to be something special. Anna, sporting her red and blue *Uff Da* apron, carefully spooned thick buttermilk pancake batter into the round depressions in the cast iron aebleskiver pan, coaxed a tablespoon of her homemade applesauce into each and waited for the batter to begin bubbling. At just the right moment, Anna deftly inserted a teaspoon and flipped each pastry over. Conrad called Anna's crowning breakfast achievement "Norwegian eyeballs." Tryg noted with satisfaction the requisite condiments on the table: Eva Gates chokecherry and huckleberry syrups and for Conrad, a fresh quarter-pound block of butter. Despite his impatience, Tryg knew better than to start a serious discussion during breakfast. He'd have to wait until the dishes were done.

Outside the small log cabin, the early morning fog was just lifting over McGregor Lake. The last embers on the fireplace hearth glowed a dull orange; the early morning fire had warmed the cabin. Tryg especially loved this time of day, watching the fog lift magically over a mirrored lake. But he was still sleepy from collecting bugs late into the night.

Tryg showered and dressed quickly while the Norwegian eyeballs turned golden brown. Anna smiled as she placed seven perfect steaming morsels onto a platter and placed them in the warming oven while seven new dollops of batter sizzled into the depressions, soon to begin bubbling. Conrad was already seated at the dining room table, sipping strong coffee from his favorite cobalt blue mug as the platter of aebleskivers and Tryg arrived. They joined hands at the round pine table, heads bowed, reciting in unison:

God is great; God is good.
Let us thank him for our food.
By his kindness all are fed.
Give us now our daily bread.
Amen

Grace was instantly followed by Conrad's booming incantation, *"Alium furiosum momentum voluptatis!"* Conrad's translation: "One mad rush of pleasure after another." With his characteristically infectious enthusiasm, Conrad spouted either the Latin or the English paraphrase at sundry celebratory occasions: setting a hook in a particularly fine trout; receiving an invitation to speak ("Anomalies of the Gallbladder") at a medical conference in Christ Church, New Zealand; romping in the bedroom with Anna, and of course, expressing appreciation of Anna's gustatory excellence (meat loaf, huckleberry pie and cinnamon rolls always earned the Latin encomium).

"Trygve Shane Lindstrom!" Anna scolded, as the youngster licked the last streaks of purple and red from his plate.

"What a naughty boy," his father laughed, raising his own plate to his lips.

Anna cleared the table, mumbling something about impossible male behavior as Conrad settled into his chair, feet resting on the ottoman, with an appreciative deep sigh, settling his pipe comfortably between his teeth. Anna allowed no indoor smoking, but Conrad was content to lean back, the old bent briarwood nestled in his large hand, ready to read the latest medical journal. As Anna settled the final dish in the drainer, Tryg impatiently went on the offensive, commandeering one side of the ottoman and facing his father. "Dad," he said, with all the adult seriousness he could muster, "I need to have a serious discussion with you and Mom."

Conrad tried not to smile, a feat made more difficult when he glanced at Anna, hands over her face trying to suppress her impulse to chuckle. How could their young son behave so, well, so endearingly grown up, so impossibly serious? Conrad respected his son's precocious intensity and was loath to give any impression of amusement. Tryg seemed not to know how to just be a kid. He had frequently summoned his parents for a "serious discussion." Conrad thought of that late night when his son, then five had suddenly bounced on their bed asking, "Is Christmas Eve morning an oxymoron?" When they had laughed, their son, hands firmly placed on hips, issued a fiery scolding.

"O.K., son. Let's reassemble at the table."

"Dear," Conrad called out to Anna as she hung up her apron. "We need to have a family meeting."

Anna's had to turn away to stifle a smile. She knew better than to look at Conrad who was certain to wink or smirk to elicit her delighted laughter. Both parents had become accustomed to Tryg's importunate *family meetings*. Among his chosen topics: proposing a fundraising sidewalk stand with lemonade and his mother's famous lingonberry scones (the effort raised nearly eight dollars for Tryg, although it cost Anna two dollars just for the berries); announcing his new career as poet and his intention to be a future poet laureate; imploring his parents to move to a large city with museums and a large library (thoughtfully suggesting three "splendid choices": Washington D.C., New York City and Boston); changing his name to Jim or Erik or Dave instead of his grandfather's cumbersome moniker; arguing for the educational benefits of owning a boa constrictor.

Tryg considered the sidewalk sale a grand success, converting his profits into a nice collection of cigar boxes purchased from Mike's Drug and Fountain where his brother got an employee discount. His favorite was a wooden box currently housing two black swallowtail butterflies. He had also won a victory with both parents voicing approval of their son's poetry aspiration, Anna presenting him with his first journal. Unfortunately, his plan for the family's move to a large city fell on deaf ears. Tryg's name change was tabled until his 21st birthday, when he could decide for himself. Anna nearly screamed in horror at Tryg's proposition to acquire a large reptile. She still shuddered at the memory of last year's escape of five garter snakes from the picnic basket to the back seat of the family automobile.

The family was now seated again at the table. Tryg stood up. "Mother and Father," he announced, "I've made up my mind. I'm going to be an entomologist. I decided earlier this summer when we went fishing in Benson's Meadow. But I need a lot of help. I'm tired of collecting bugs like a kid. I'm using cigar boxes for insect cases. I've got the wrong kind of pins and pinning boards. I'm using moth balls to preserve my specimens--it's ruined the wings of some of my butterflies and moths." Tryg seemed to be warming to his subject, becoming increasingly animated. "And, I just don't have enough books! There's no one in Libby who's a real entomologist, not even Mr. Anderson (the high school science teacher). Our county library has two great books--Holland's book on moths and his other one on butterflies. The librarian lets me keep them all summer. Zero books on beetles; zero on wasps; zero on flies, zero on crickets. It does have Comstock's spider book, but I don't like spiders and his book is practically unreadable. How can I find out the scientific names of my specimens? It's pitiful!

And my *Field Guide to Western Insects*! It's pretty much useless. Three out of four insects in my collection aren't in the book."

Tears suddenly welled up in Tryg's eyes. "I want to go to Bozeman or Missoula to visit entomologists at the university--if they even have entomologists there. I want to go to the Smithsonian and to the Museum of Natural History in New York. I want to see the great insect collections. I'm tired of collecting like a, a," his voice cracked with emotion, "like an amateur, like a . . . kid!"

The boy sat down, breathing deeply. His cheeks were flushed but he showed no embarrassment for the tears that streaked his face. There was a moment of silence while Tryg took a few deep breaths. Anna looked at Conrad with some kind of silent signal demanding his response.

Anna and Conrad sat in silence for a minute while Tryg composed himself. He had spoken his piece. He expected nothing less than his parents' full support. Both struggled mightily not to smile and avoided looking at one another. Their son, so endearing, so deadly serious; they knew how important this moment was to him. Conrad spoke first: "Son, I know you'll be a great entomologist. You've shown resolve, patience, ingenuity: buying your own cigar boxes, poring over Holland's butterfly book, and already putting together an impressive collection of bugs. Your mother and I are very proud of you. Here's what we're going to do. We'll buy you the professional equipment you need: spreading boards, entomologist's pins, insect cases, a real butterfly net. I don't know exactly what you should have, but we'll find out. There must be some kind of safe chemical to use to kill your specimens--cyanide's way too dangerous. At some point you'll probably need a dissecting microscope and a camera. To me, all of these preparations are part of your education. We'll find out what entomologists use for dispatching fluid; there must be safe killing jars and we need to find out how to preserve your insects. You start writing letters to museums—keep a copy of each letter for your journals. When you find someone willing to talk to you, we'll pay him a visit. We'll find time to take a trip to New York and Washington D.C. There's got to be a great collection of Montana insects in Bozeman or Missoula. Spokane may have a museum and it's only a four-hour train ride away. The Natural History Museum in Denver is supposed to be one of the best. We could drive there and go through Yellowstone on the way. Or we could fly from Kalispell.

"Son, I want to say one more thing to you. You *are* an amateur. A true amateur. And I hope you'll always have the courage to be one. Amateur means *lover*. It means you study with your heart as well as with your brain. You don't just study insects. You love the darn critters. It's easy to become a scientist. But an *amateur*! I want you to understand and respect that word."

It was Tryg's turn to be silent. He sat erect and motionless, face turning red, tears rolling down his face.

His only journal entry for that day:

Trygve Shane Lindstrom
***Amateur* Entomologist**.

12

The Smithsonian (Tryg, age 11)

In Flanders Fields the poppies blow
Between the crosses row on row

John McCrae
"In Flander's Field"

Dr. Lindstrom couldn't believe how difficult it had been to gain access to the Smithsonian's archival insect collection. For months his son's persistent letters had met with an increasingly upsetting silence. He could understand a polite rejection of his son's request, but to cavalierly ignore him. Unacceptable! Conrad secretly penned his own animated letters which, to his chagrin, were similarly ignored. He couldn't understand it. Wasn't the Smithsonian a public institution, supported by public taxes? He had waited long enough. He jerked the phone off the hook and made two calls. The first was to the U.S. Senator from Montana he had supported in two successful elections. The second was to Forrest Maxwell, U.S. Surgeon General, with whom he had co-authored an article on the effects of tremolite on lung disease.

Tryg bounded into the living room, waving the handsome linen envelope, a bright red Smithsonian "Castle" embossed in the corner. "Dad! We've been invited to the Smithsonian! Get this, quote: 'With full academic privileges to the library and all museum archives.'" The envelope included two name badges and instructions for affixing passport photos to them. "*Alium furiosum momentum voluptatis*!" he shouted with glee.

The Smithsonian Museum of Natural History. By now, Conrad was used to the museum drill—Tryg led the way, his father just there for the ride. But this time, Conrad was surprised: his son had scarcely glanced at the insect cases displayed on the wall, and Tryg even gave the live insect zoo a brief unengaged visit. They had spent most of the morning looking at gems and minerals, then browsing through the gift shop while Tryg kept checking the time. At a minute before noon, Tryg impatiently tugged his father to the visitor desk where Dr. Toppen was waiting as promised. The octogenarian Curator of Invertebrates looked carefully at his guests' security badges and escorted them silently through secured doors to the hallowed space housing tens of millions of specimens. Under the guardian's watchful eye, Tryg opened drawer after drawer of preserved, pinned and labeled beetles. Thousands of perfectly aligned six-foot oak Cornell-drawer cabinets stretched for hundreds of feet, row upon narrow row. Tryg gave each drawer a cursory glance, asking to see *Plusiotis* beetles, then *Macrodontias*, or *Callipogons*. The curator dutifully located each request, seemingly unimpressed by the precocious young entomologist under his care. After an hour, Tryg unexpectedly said he was finished.

Outside, walking along the Mall, Conrad finally asked his son about the tour.

"I hated it, Dad," he announced. "It *was* perfect," he said stumbling to find the right words. "A perfect graveyard, just like the Arlington

Cemetery. They have more than 500 copies of *Acrocinus longimanus*—big ones, little ones, pink ones, red ones, orange ones, even a few purple ones. I doubt if there's a single scientist in the world who will ever make any use of those 500 beetles, locked away in a warehouse with millions of other bugs. I know it's an important collection, but I don't want to look at drawers filled with hundreds of the same wasp or earwig. And did you see that curator guy? Boris Karloff would have been a friendlier host. He doesn't love that collection. He just guards it. You'd think he'd say, "Hey kid, want to see something really cool. Let me show you this." A good day's work for him is when the doors stay locked the entire day and no one disturbs the place. He's a stereotype of the librarian who hates it when people check out her books. He is not an amateur!

"Remember the May Museum in Colorado Springs?" His dad just nodded, smiling. "Now that was a cool museum, and you could tell Mr. May just loved showing things to me. Like the tarantula with the bird in its jaws. Or the huge stick insect with tiny legs on one side and normal ones on the other. Or the stag beetle with his eyes divided in half horizontally. He even asked me why I thought the eyes were made that way. It's a great question and I still don't know the answer. I wonder if he knows. I'd go back there in a second. He just loves his morpho butterflies and metallic beetles.

"And did you see the display of insects the Smithsonian puts on for the public! It's pitiful. Fourteen lousy cases. There are more species of insects in the world than all other animals combined. And they display only 14 cases. Where is the biggest beetle in the world? Not on display. How about a huge centipede or scorpion or other creepy things. They don't have the best stuff on display, just some examples of each family. Where's the giant African wasp nest or the most colorful butterflies? They don't even have a moon moth! And their living zoo of bugs and spiders is lame too. They have only four tarantulas and none of the cool ones like the iridescent spiders from Thailand. And no goliath spider! Hissing cockroaches—big deal. Every insect zoo has 'em.

"They should have *stories*. If they put me in charge, I'd have a huge museum dedicated to invertebrates."

Conrad laughed at his son's tirade. "Come on, Sport," he said. "Let's get a burger and a malt. You're way too young to be so jaded. I want you to tell me what the Trygve Lindstrom Invertebrate Museum would be like."

The taxi driver knew the perfect place—Uncle John's Malt Shop in Georgetown. They both ordered an Uncle John (half-pound Angus beef burger with Tillamook cheddar cheese), Ghirardelli dark chocolate malt (extra malty) and old-fashioned fries (skin on). Even at 2:30 the place was packed, mostly with students poring over open textbooks.

"O.K., son, "tell me how you'd make a better museum."

"Well," Tryg started, his brow furrowed as he marshalled his thoughts. "You know, Dad. We've been to a lot of museums together. I always like to see minerals and shells. Seems like they always have the best stuff on display. Everyone wants to see the Hope diamond. So far, nobody except the May Museum has had a great display of bugs. Those diorama things—they kinda give me the creeps. Somebody spends a million hours making every blade of grass and yet it still looks fake. The painted backgrounds are cheesy. If you take a photograph, everyone can see right away it's not real. The little stuffed birds are kind of pitiful. I'm not having any dioramas in my museum, that's for sure.

"I guess the main thing is, my museum would be a place for the public—for people who want to learn and see stuff. No rows of cases behind locked doors. For sure, no 500 copies of the same cricket. I guess we need collections like that, although I'm not really sure why. People like to see the biggest and the spookiest, the things that bite and sting. They want to see a live tarantula or a huge walking sick. They want to see birdwing butterflies and morphos and Atlas moths. How's this for an idea: a butterfly house with lots of live butterflies, a place you can walk through. People want to see displays that look like works of art—and the really curious ones want to read, you know, interesting stuff, like how bees keep a hive warm in winter or how termites air condition their huge mounds, or how bombardier beetles squirt chemicals to defend themselves.

"I'd have lots of live things: hissing cockroaches of course—everybody has those, but tons more—like goliath spiders. If there were a *Guinness Book of World Records* for bugs, I'd have 'em all on display, like *Pandinus imperator*, the biggest scorpion. I'd have the world's biggest beetle, moth, bumblebee, dragonfly. Oh yeah, how about a fossil of a three-foot dragonfly like we saw in Colorado? Did you know there's a cricket in New Zealand that's 15 centimeters long? Wouldn't you love to see a six-foot long worm? Or a clam that weighs a ton? Maybe even some models of other huge prehistoric insects like a two-foot-long cockroach. We'd have termite colonies and wasp nests and honeybees. How about an active mud dauber nest and a huge communal orb-weaver spider web like we saw yesterday at the National Zoo? My museum would be," he paused for a moment, 'exciting.' There's more to entomology than putting bugs in really straight lines in thousands of matching drawers, and then putting thousands of cabinets in more straight lines. Nicholas and my friend Alex are the only ones I know who would have loved seeing the rows of cabinets.

"I'd have lots of big color displays and short films. I'd show people how mud daubers paralyze spiders and build nests of mud. I'd show them a ten-foot-tall termite mound with a perfect system of air conditioning. I'd show them a female praying mantis eating her mate or snatching a fly out of the air. Cool stuff, creepy stuff, amazing stuff. And of course, I'd have a display of the monarch migrating from Canada to California!

"And here's another thing." Tryg was starting to warm again to his subject, becoming more animated as he was able to verbalize his feelings. "I'd have a museum shop with real stuff instead of all the junk they sell. Of all the museums we've been to, name one that sold real insect pins or spreading boards." Before Conrad proffered his educated guess, Tryg interjected, "Not one! It's even hard to find a real butterfly net. Not one single museum shop we've visited has insect cases or dried specimens for sale. We have to order them by mail from Brooklyn. They have dopey little-kid insect nets and models of rubber bugs. Even the Smithsonian doesn't sell professional insect pins or setting boards or even a decent microscope. Not a single dissecting microscope. My museum will teach people how to raise praying mantises or care for a tarantula. We'll go on collecting trips. We'll learn about insect behavior. Maybe we'll take nature trips to Costa Rica or Madagascar. Maybe that's what I want to do . . . create my own museum. And you know what, Father? Everybody who works in my museum is going to be an amateur."

They both laughed, dipping fries into their malts.

In the next few years, he and his parents visited eleven major museums including the British Museum of Natural History when he was 16. Tryg would never forget that trip. His father had been sick all winter, coughing through the night. But nothing was going to interfere with a personal tour of the British Museum insect collection. Tryg took a gift to the museum: more than a hundred specimens of Montana insects, including the solitary wood-boring ant he had discovered and named *Formicans conradi*.

While other tourists visited the Tower of London and Buckingham Palace, Tryg and Conrad spent their precious three days looking at countless thousands of invertebrates and drinking tea with eminent British entomologists who treated the young man as a colleague. After all, Tryg had already published five articles on insect behavior, including his observations of hunting wasps in *Nature*.

He would never forget those days in London with his father. It was the last trip they'd ever take together.

13

The Big Game Hunter
(Tryg, age 12)

He lifts the Tube, and levels with his Eye;
Strait a short Thunder breaks the frozen Sky.

Alexander Pope
"Hunting and Fishing"

When I tell stories about growing up in Libby, most people seem surprised by the freedoms we enjoyed back then as well as the responsibilities placed on us. Father gave me a .22 rifle when I was seven. I was just one of many young boys with a .22. I spent hours alone on McGreggor Lake in our 12-foot boat. Along with Nicholas I split and stacked wood for the cabin's fireplace. When I turned ten, I was allowed to use the chainsaw. In the deep of winter, I took my turn padding down to the basement, chopping sections of a Pres-to-Log and maintaining the fire in the furnace.

I loved my Remington Model 514, single shot, bolt action .22, with a real walnut wood stock. It cost $15.40 brand new, plus $1.05 shipping. Most weeks I happily spent my dollar allowance on two boxes of .22 long rifle shells. Nicholas had a lovely Marlin 39-A lever-action .22 and I expected to "grow into" a similar semi-automatic rifle when I was a bit older. This beauty was much more expensive: $60.85. The one animal universally approved for killing was the gopher. Gophers endangered cattle, who were prone to stepping into a hole and injuring themselves, often having to be put down, so ranchers offered the handsome sum of one dollar per gopher carcass. One really good day I earned four dollars.

My friends and I were all adept with our rifles. We each had our own cleaning kits, with cleaning rod (threading the two pieces together), small circles of white felt, solvent and oil. We kept the barrels immaculate, cleaned after every practice, wooden stocks kept shiny with oil, and we maintained a near religious zeal for the rules of safety. To my knowledge, no person in Libby has ever been killed or injured by an accident with a firearm. We became sharpshooters by practice, practice, practice. The first targets were tin cans, readily available at the dump across Highway 2. We'd gather as many as we could carry to "Shooter's Hill," where we lined up the cans on a log in front of the steep embankment. We invented our own hierarchy. Beginners lay on the ground, resting their rifles on sandbags. At 25 yards, the sandbag shoot was ridiculously easy, and the youngest shooters quickly became greenhorns. The next and much more difficult challenge was firing from a standing position without any support. The trick was trying to hold the rifle rock steady. Ten consecutive hits earned promotion to frontiersman. Level three shooters, marksmen, turned the cans on their sides and aimed at the bottoms from 30 yards. Every boy I know soon became a marksman, routinely hitting 10 cans in a row from a standing position.

Sharpshooter was the gold standard; getting to that level cost me many weeks of allowance. First of all, we had to find pop bottles which were much harder to collect than tin cans. That accomplished, we lined up ten bottles on their sides, the openings facing us. At 40 yards we lay down, rested our rifles on a couple of sandbags and aimed ever so carefully. Each bullet had to fly through the opening of the bottle and shatter the bottom on the way out. Two boys used a 4x power scope, which some of us considered cheating, but they pointed out that most big game hunters used scopes and there was no rule against it. I didn't earn the coveted sharpshooter label until I was nine.

On my twelfth birthday, Father surprised me with a wonderful gift, a brand-new Remington bolt-action Model 721 30-06. I remember his speech, Mother staying silent, arms crossed, brow furrowed.

"Son," Father said. "I don't know if you even want to be a hunter. You know I don't hunt. Our freezer is full every winter with elk and deer, antelope and bison and sometimes even bear meat. But I'm not a hunter. I love deer and elk. I understand that many people here depend on venison to get through the winter. But we're lucky; I don't need to hunt to feed our family.

Still. I don't know a single one of your friends who doesn't hunt. You need to decide for yourself. Here's twenty dollars to buy shells and see what it feels like to fire a hunting weapon."

Across Mineral Ave from Father's clinic was the Texaco station that also sold ammunition and bartered in used pistols and rifles. Almost every week I'd buy one or two boxes of .22 shells. Now I had a chance to buy bullets for a big game rifle. Bullets come 20 to a box, so I asked for one box of shells.

"110, 150, 180 or 220 grain?" Alan asked.

I had no idea what he was talking about. So, Alan gave me my first lesson. "Grain refers to the weight of the bullet," he said, obviously pleased to be my teacher. "Those .22 shells you keep buying--they're about 40 grains. You can read about bullets and handguns and rifles in *The Shooter's Bible*. Every hunter should have this book. Tell you something very few people know," he said conspiratorially. "It takes 7,000 grains to make a pound." Alan continued with my lesson, explaining that the 125-grain bullets cost a bit less and were perfect for "varmits"--gophers for sure and rats that sneaked around the dump. Most people bought the 150-grain bullets for deer and antelope hunting and the 180-grain for elk. "I'd definitely recommend a 220-grain bullet for moose." I told Alan I'd try the 125-grain. A box of ten cartridges of any size cost $4.00. My .22 shells looked tiny next to 30-06 ammo. At forty cents a cartridge, target practice was going to be expensive.

Fortunately, I discovered that all my practice with a .22 transferred to my big game rifle. The main difference was the weight of the rifle and keeping it steady. But how wonderfully the rifle performed! At 100 yards I could aim dead center on a target and the bullet didn't drop a millimeter. With my .22, the bullet dropped a couple of inches in 100 yards and I'd have to adjust my aim accordingly. After twenty rounds I felt confident and four more dollars on a box of 180-grain shells. I had just received my elk tag in the mail; I was going for an elk.

The first week of hunting season we usually see pickups returning to Libby with deer and elk. But this year the warm autumn days lingered; big game remained higher in the Cabinets. Then it snowed. All week long the mountains faced a blizzard: lots of snow, high winds, arctic temperatures. At last elk would begin migrating into the valleys.

Six families I knew well had decided to drive up the Goose Creek Road where elk gathered every fall. You'd think the elk would learn and go somewhere else, but for decades, hunters had brought home venison from Goose Creek. Three of the hunters had managed to purchase elk tags from the annual lottery. My father's good friend, Olav, volunteered to take me on my first hunting trip. His old jeep had a rifle rack in the cab. Olav picked me up at dawn, Mother packing lunches for both of us, and we were off. Olav said he'd take me to the far end of the Goose Creek meadow, where we'd probably be alone.

As we began climbing the unpaved road, it began snowing. Olav turned on his windshield wiper, but my side of the windshield was quickly obscured. "Have to do the work yourself," Olav chuckled. The passenger-side wiper had a small handle--I had to move the handle back and forth manually to clear the windshield. We drove higher and higher; the snow got deeper and deeper. I admit to being a bit nervous, but Olav was mighty proud of his four-wheel drive Jeep as it hugged the curves. The sharp drops made me queasy. "Look," Olav said. "That's the Thompkins crew. There's Jenkins and Smitty, Zeke and Nate. They're waiting for the elk herd." We drove past.

Half an hour later we stopped. The sky was clearing. We both stepped out of the cozy Jeep into a foot of fresh snow and a bracing chill. In the afternoon, high winds often howl through the Goose Creek meadow, but thankfully the air was still and the sky now a deep, iridescent blue. Then we spotted him a handsome four-point bull elk. He was no trophy, but a large, mature bull. It was too easy. The elk stood on an exposed ridge above us, a perfect silhouette, perhaps 80 yards away. I reached into the cab, lifted my rifle and closed the bolt, seating a 180-grain bullet. I think the elk heard the click of the bolt. He turned his head toward us. I lofted my rifle and aimed just above the shoulder. Too easy. I held my breath. I began a slow squeeze of the trigger. Then I looked into the large brown eyes and lowered my rifle.

"I can't do it, Mr. Hanson, "I just can't. He's looking straight at me. He's, well, he's beautiful." My voice was choking. I could feel my eyes welling with tears and my cheeks burning with shame. Olav started laughing.

"You're as bad as your dad," Olav said. "Doc'll never be a hunter and I reckon you'll never be one either. Empty your gun and let's go home."

The elk watched us get into the Jeep and start back down the road.

Half an hour later we returned to the lower meadow. Six trucks had gathered in a semi-circle, men in coats and orange vests. It was the Thompkins crew. They had made a kill. We drove closer. Three bull elk lay on the ground within a few yards of each other. Olav and I got out and greeted the men. Nate was already gutting one of the animals, steam rising from his belly. Six families could look forward to a supply of venison all winter. Random impressions:

Three beautiful elk, lying on the snow.
Large vacant brown eyes.
Tongues lolling.
Zeke getting his photo taken, holding up an antlered head.
Crimson-stained snow.
Passing around the flask of whiskey.
But my most vivid memory: steam rising from warm bodies.

"Hey kid," Zeke called out. "This summer, my Jenny broke her arm something terrible. Thought she might even lose it. Doc fixed her up pretty good. She can even use her hand again. I bet Doc likes jerky--make it myself. It'll be ready for Christmas; I'll stop by."

I think I mumbled a quiet thanks, still trying to deal with the slaughter. Olav was right. I'm as bad as my father; I'll never be a hunter. That night I talked to Father. I wanted to sell my rifle and my Marlin lever action .22. I was done with target shooting. I was done with rifles. But I had an idea, a great idea. The next day Father called the Sons of Norway store in Spokane.

14

Ice Capades
(Tryg, age 12)

Loose to the wind their airy garments flew,
Thin glittering textures of the filmy dew,
Dipt in the richest tincture of the skies,
Where light disports in ever mingling dyes,
While every beam new transient colours flings,
Colours that change whene'er they wave their wings.

Alexander Pope
Rape of the Lock

Christmas was over. Father sat in his favorite chair, reminiscing on the bountiful feast and showering praise on Mother, whose green eyes sparkled. Anna's turkey was perfect, and she had made plenty of gravy. Father always worried that we might run out. His mashed potatoes and cornmeal stuffing always swam in gravy, and he looked forward to reheating the leftovers. Mother had made her special cranberry-lingonberry sauce. We had the essential Norwegian side dishes: pickled herring, pickled beets, cucumber slices in vinegar and sugar. Oh, the cookies, cookies, cookies: frosted sugar cookies (my favorite), anise cookies (for Nicholas), shortbread wedding cake cookies drenched in powdered sugar (for Mother), pizzelles, biscotti (Father's choice, to be dunked in strong coffee). Father made a cookie sheet of glorious semisweet chocolate fudge. Mother baked huckleberry pie from her stash of frozen berries, served with plenty of ice cream, along with pecan and pumpkin pies. The next-door neighbor brought us her signature lemon bars.

Father pronounced it to be the best Christmas dinner we had ever had. Father's assessment was both mandatory and expected, but Mother still beamed. After dinner, Mother and Father sipped aquavit, for the first time letting me sample the vile, burning stuff. It's our tradition to open stockings on Christmas Eve morning and presents on Christmas Day. It wasn't easy waiting. First, we all went to church. Then mother was busy in the kitchen. When the turkey had cooled a bit, father carved, setting aside a leg for me (Nicholas and mother favoring white meat). We listened to all six of our Christmas records at least five times. After dinner (Mother insisting that she first wash the dishes and clean the kitchen) we *finally* gather in the living room, her three men trying to conceal their impatience. The pies and fudge and lemon bars wait until all the presents have been opened *and* the living room cleared of boxes and wrapping paper.

Nicholas got two presents that I remember. The first was a coupon good for a three-piece suit. Father had his suits made to measure. At 6' 5" he needed to be fitted. Even his shoes (14 AAA) had to be specially ordered. Father said it was time for Nicholas to have a professional suit. After all, he was now nineteen, already determined to attend graduate school at Purdue. Nicholas already wore a white shirt and tie to every class. I hope Mother and Father knew better than to buy me a suit! Nicholas also received something he called "the best gift I've ever been given:" a handsome black leather box stamped "Kopernikus IX" in gold letters. What a fine insect box it would have made. Inside was a 17-piece set of drafting compasses, made in Germany, each fitted into custom fitted depressions in the red felt. It was of course the perfect present for my brother--each piece, beautifully crafted and housed in its own place. The compasses were brass, equipped with little dials for the most precise settings. Other pieces were extensions. One small tube held replacement graphite. What wonderfully perfect circles my brother could now draw!

My most memorable present was a big heavy box that I opened last. Sixteen yellow books: *The New Illustrated Animal Kingdom*. Right away I noticed that volumes 12 -15 were labelled, "Insects." Oh joy! I opened volume 15 to page 1824 (wow! page 1824). There was a picture of a water beetle with the title, "Biters and Killers." Even the lure of huckleberry pie ala mode vanished (temporarily) as I began reading:

> *When one of these water bugs seizes another insect or even a fish, it jabs the captive again and again with its beak while holding on with its powerful front legs. The more the victim struggles, the tighter the front legs close.*
>
> *Fishes up to five inches long can be killed by one of these three-inch bugs. A number of them in fish-hatchery pools can do considerable damage, making serious pests of themselves.*

I continued reading until Mother insisted I put down my book and join the family. Suddenly dessert sounded pretty good. Mother explained that she had seen my set of books at Duncan's a year ago and had it sent to Libby where the box had remained hidden in her closet for nearly a year.

I stayed up all night reading. Who wouldn't have.

We all knew that the day after Christmas was the time to plan our annual trip to Spokane; most years it was our only family vacation. Mother loved the Ice Capades in Spokane and the trip was now an entrenched family tradition. Every year Mother speculated that this might be the last time the four of us would be together. Nicholas was finishing his sophomore year of college, majoring in math of course.

I loved the trip to Spokane, staying at the Ridpath, shopping for a new book at Duncan's, a wonderful huge two-story bookstore, strolling in the big city with its tall buildings and department stores. For Mother, the Ice Capades was the highlight of the trip and her "three boys," well, we humored Mother. Of course, we did! I remember so many details about our trips to Spokane. First of all, we enjoyed the four-hour train ride on the Great Northern Railway Empire Builder, watching the Kootenai from the Vistadome. Special treats included a baked apple with brown sugar syrup or hot apple pie with soft cheddar cheese that came in a little brown crock.

To me everything seemed wonderful in Spokane. The cab ride from the train station to the Ridpath. Dinner on the top of the Ridpath, where they carved roast beef at the table from a giant hooded cart. Nicholas and I could pick out any book we wanted at Duncan's

Every year, Mother visited the Sons of Norway store. She'd admire the blue and white dishes, the wall hangings, laugh at carved wooden gnomes and trolls, pause over framed photographs of fjords, admire objects of pewter and silver and crystal. But she always stopped a bit longer at the jewelry case at one particular display on black silk in a cherrywood box: a jade pendant, earrings and ring. Each was set in delicate silver filigree. Each year she sighed, relieved to see the jewelry still on display.

We could count on her to buy something: a sterling silver cheese slicer or an apron, a Christmas tree ornament or at the very least an *Uff Da* bumper sticker. But she always lingered at the silver and jade treasure lying in the cherrywood box.

Two nights in Spokane. French toast for breakfast. Riding up and down the elevator just for fun. Father spending a whole dollar on a cigar that came in its own metal tube with a screw cap, the cigar wrapped in a thin sheet of cedar. (Yep, the tube's in my cabinet). Pizza for lunch. (Even Kalispell didn't yet have a pizza parlor). Prime rib dinner on the Ridpath Roof Restaurant. The Ice Capades matinee. Dinner the next night at the Davenport where I ordered a crab cocktail followed by shish kabob brought flaming to the table. Oh, the wonderfulness, the elegance, the excess of it all! And finally, the four-hour train trip back to Libby, trying to spot mountain goats on the cliffs or a herd of elk along the river.

This trip was a little different. When we arrived in Spokane, the four of us squeezed into the cab, bundled in our heavy coats. Father sat in the front seat and told the driver to make a stop at The Davenport, three blocks away from the Ridpath, where we were staying. Mother registered a puzzled look but said nothing. We boys stared straight ahead in studied Norwegian stoicism.

Father got out of the cab and instructed the driver to take us to our hotel. He told Mother he had something to do and would join us a bit later.

Father returned while Mother was still unpacking. She always insisted on putting clothes in the dresser and closet. Nicholas and I had an adjoining bedroom; Nicholas was busy placing his underwear on the left side of a drawer, then two pair of neatly folded socks on the right. Me? I didn't see the point. I put my suitcase on the folding luggage rack in the closet where I could easily find whatever clothes I needed. What a waste of time folding underwear and socks!

Mother was eager to walk around town; Nicholas and I could hardly wait to visit Duncan's to buy a book. So, the three of us took off. Father said he'd just like to relax in the Ridpath lounge. The Minnesota Gophers had finally enjoyed a winning season and the bowl game was going to be televised.

First stop, of course, Duncan's. I already knew the book I wanted, Jack London's *White Fang*. After reading Father's copy of *Call of the Wild*, I had to read another London book. Father suggested I wait a couple of years before reading *The Sea Wolf*. Nicholas found a book about Lewis and Clark, one with maps. That was about the only thing my brother and I had in common: our love of maps.

The three of us strolled together, stopping at The Davenport. This year the lobby displayed domed wire birdcages, with little songbirds, finches and bluebirds and lorikeets. I couldn't help but feel sorry for them. The huge fireplace had a welcoming yule log. We took a table in the Peacock Lounge, and each ordered a sundae: (mine caramel, Mother, hot fudge, Nicholas, hot fudge with the fudge on the side! Was there ever a more annoying brother?).

We continued our walk as it began snowing. Windows were still decorated with colored lights and Santas and moving toy trains. Even though Christmas was over, "Joy to the World" filled the air from an unseen speaker. We couldn't resist buying a bag of roasted chestnuts from a sidewalk vendor. When we arrived at Sons of Norway, Nicholas opened the door for Mother; we were as familiar with this mandatory stop as our annual pilgrimage to Duncan's. Nicholas and I discovered beautiful knives, some with wooden handles, others with handles of antler horn. Mother wandered around the familiar room, handling dish towels, then looking at the latest edition of a Norwegian Christmas display plate. When she gravitated toward the jewelry case, we studiously renewed our interest in the knives.

Mother stopped at the case and stared. She seemed to shrink a little. A shopkeeper asked if she liked the display. "Lovely," she answered in a flat tone.

"It's genuine Swarovski crystal," he said. "I think the creche is just beautiful. It's specially priced for the season," he added hopefully.

We left the store without making a purchase. Back in our room Father was in a grand mood; the Gophers had won their football game. Nicholas and I showed off our new books. Mother reminded us that our dinner reservations were at 6:30; let's all be ready in time.

That night the four of us sat by a window in the Ridpath Roof Restaurant in burgundy upholstered chairs watching the snow falling and staring at people walking 12 stories below us. The waiters wore black vests, white shirts and bright red bow ties. Each table glowed by candlelight. A string quartet played in the corner. The tablecloth and napkins were burgundy linen, matching our chairs. Each place setting had three forks! The waiter ground Parmesan cheese over our Caesar salads and then pepper from a two-foot-long pepper mill. Dinner was a performance. I pretended that we were a royal family, visiting from Europe. Finally, the celebrated prime rib cart arrived, the waiter opening the curved silver top with a flourish. Mother and I asked for medium; Father preferred rare, and Nicholas asked for the very end cut (anything to be different). When the plates were cleared and the dessert menus arrived, Father said he had an announcement to make. Father isn't very good at announcements and speeches. I'm the talker in the family. But Father, to his credit, did a pretty good job (for Father).

"Anna," he said. "Your three boys wanted to make this Christmas season extra special. We have another present for you, a few days late."

That was his entire speech: for Father, a noteworthy rhetorical achievement. He stood up, producing a beautifully wrapped rectangular box and placed it in front of Mother. He sheepishly (and unnecessarily) admitted that the store clerk had wrapped the gift. Father is notoriously inept at wrapping presents. You'd think a surgeon would be adept at such things, but he's hopeless and his personally wrapped gifts invariably evoke good-humored laughter around the Christmas tree. I take after Father in this regard. Mother just stared at the box. "Did you stop at Duncan's to get me that bird book?" she asked.

"Open it, Mother!" I blurted impatiently, as Father chuckled and sat down again.

Mother and Nicholas have one thing in common: they employ a most annoying method of opening presents. Mother fussed with the tape until she could peel it back, careful not to tear the paper. She unfolded each fold, smoothing out the shiny blue foil paper. Her excruciatingly cautious process ensured that the wrapping could be used another day. Father and I have a much different approach, a much more satisfying technique, leaving paper and ribbons in shreds. We get down to business, going on the offensive, liberating a present in record time. Opening a present should be in itself a celebration, performed with exuberance. Mother continued at her own pace, Father and I fairly bursting with impatience. Nicholas smiled approvingly. Nicholas and Mother conspire to make Father and me squirm. At long last, blue foil paper unfolded and smoothed, the unveiling revealed a shiny red cherrywood box. Mother uttered a quiet, "Oh." Then came the tears. Hers . . . and then mine. She gently lifted the cover to reveal four jade treasures, displayed on black silk, practically glowing in the candlelight. A small silver plate read:

Magnus Magnussen
Silversmith, Jeweler
Oslo, Norge

I had labored over a poem for the occasion. I wanted my poem to sound "grown up" and "important" like the renaissance poets in books Mother had given me, Shakespeare and Ben Jonson and Wyatt. How proud I was to use words like "thee" and "Zephyrus." Something kept me from giving it to Mother until we returned to Libby.

To Mother

How freshly green, our love's for thee,
Green as the tend'rist shoots of spring,
Fragile as Zephyrus' sweetest showers
Or lullabies young mothers sing.

Green, oh green, yet purpose driven
Determined, ever finds a way;
Reaching, grasping for the sun
Green drives love closer every day.

Awakened by illumined glow
Are lessons we've been learning;
It gives us joy to give to you
These objects of your yearning.

Let green be your defining color,
Emerald green to match your eyes.
From three men who thee adore,
Gentle, beautiful and wise.

From the three men in your life

Cinnamon rolls *had* to be in our near future.
Father insisted we end the evening with dessert. Our waiter suggested raspberries flambee, the specialty of the house. Father immediately assented, "flambee" sounding exciting and raspberries being a special

favorite of Mother. Another cart (accompanied by two black vests with red bow toes) rolled to our table, laden with wonderful things: a large silver dish with butter, just beginning to melt above a blue flame, two bottles of spirits, a bowl of ice cream, another bowl heaped with brown sugar, half a lemon, assorted utensils. The dessert chef deftly folded the mound of brown sugar into the melted butter. A pint of ripe raspberries joined the mixture, gently stirred, then drenched in raspberry liquor. Next, the chef squeezed half a fresh lemon, wrapped in cheesecloth, ("To trap any seeds," Father explained). Finally, brandy was drizzled over the entire exotic concoction. The chef tilted the pan to the flame and the mixture burst into a lovely blue flame. I'm sure everyone in the room was watching. Would father burst into his Latin phrase? While we had been entranced by melting and pouring, stirring, squeezing and enflaming, dishes of vanilla ice cream had appeared in front of each of us. The chef spooned the still flaming mixture over the ice cream. Ice cream twice in one day! Raspberries flambee were even more delicious than my caramel sundae. As each of us savored the ecstasy, Father announced that Anna's cinnamon rolls were still at the peak of Mount Everest, but raspberries flambee had ascended, in his estimation, to K-2. Who could have possibly imagined Father could speak in such eloquent metaphors. Raspberries flambee can evoke such inspiration.

Back in Libby several days later I noticed an empty shelf on Nicholas' side of the bedroom. His four hand-built wooden tall ships were missing. I asked Father if Nicholas had taken them to college with him.

"Nicholas sold them, son. It was his contribution to Anna's gift."

Maybe Nicholas isn't the worst brother in the world after all.

15

Tryg on Trial
(Tryg, age 13)

Ye shall know the truth and the truth will set you free.

John 8:32

When Mrs. Anderson announced details of the freshman research paper, most of the class groaned. In Libby schools, report cards came out every six weeks called "terms." The major assignment would count for a daunting 50 percent of the first term grade. "Welcome to high school," Mrs. Anderson said with a smile. Students had to submit a topic for her approval. The paper had to be at least 3,000 words (Count on Alex to meet that number on the dot). Quoted material must be footnoted, giving credit to the author; bibliography at the end of the paper. "Your paper has to be written in pen (not pink or lavender, girls) and *must be legible,*" she added. Tryg feared "legible" might pose a challenge. "If any of you have a typewriter, so much the better," she added hopefully. At last, Tryg could write about insects, and get credit! He decided to write on mud daubers. He could use quotes from the Fabre book his father had given him, and maybe a paragraph from a well-worn issue of *National Geographic Magazine* as well as an entry from the home library's *Encyclopedia Britannica*. He had already written many journal pages of his own observations and could even add his own speculation about what he had called the "cuckoo wasp." Papers were due in a month, just two weeks before the end of the first six-week term. Maybe he could include a mud dauber poem.

Tryg loved his English class. Mrs. Anderson started each class with a puzzle or riddle.

> *Two common U.S. coins amount to 26 cents. One coin is not a quarter. What are the two coins?*

Mrs. Anderson chuckled when she gave the answer: "The two coins are a quarter and a penny. I said that *one* coin was not a quarter. But the *other* coin *is* a quarter.

Mrs. Anderson started every day with a "Building my Vocabulary" word on the blackboard followed by a complicated sentence for diagramming. Students had a few minutes to diagram the challenging sentence and also use the word of the day "intelligently," showing they understood the word. "If the word is *lemur*," Mrs. Anderson warned with a smile, "don't you dare submit *I saw a lemur*. Your sentence must clearly show you know the *meaning* of the word." Each day, Mrs. Anderson enjoyed sharing a few student sentences. Today's word: *patella*.

> Sheila: "Last Sunday at mass, I had to kneel on my patellas six times."

> Ben: "I saw a patella. Just kidding, Mrs. Anderson! How's this: I remember how much it hurt when I fell and bumped my patella. My knee hurt all day."

Tryg wrote a poetic couplet. Self-conscious about the rhyme, he added, "In the style of Ogden Nash."

> *I dropped an egg yolk on my patella*
> *My kneecap's sticky, wet and yella.*

Yes, English class was fun. For several days the class moved into the school library, students thumbing through the card catalog, opening encyclopedias, seeking the librarian's help to find magazine articles on their topics. Students were encouraged to use the county library as well. Tryg found nothing useful on mud dauber wasps. But he had plenty to write about; his paper would be much longer than the minimum.

But there was a problem. Mrs. Anderson was pregnant. She called herself "very pregnant." When she stood, she had to hold her prominent belly with both hands. Everyone knew a baby was coming very soon, hopefully not in the classroom! Finally, she announced she was taking maternity leave and wouldn't return until second semester. She'd be gone for three months. A substitute teacher, Mrs. Griseldi, would be taking over the class and grading the research papers.

Mrs. Griseldi arrived. Older. Serious. Maybe she'd be a good teacher, Tryg thought, but class wasn't going to be nearly as much fun. No daily riddle or puzzle. No sentence to diagram, no word of the day. Students turned in their research masterpieces and Mrs. Griseldi started a new unit for second term: the short story. The first short story was "Gift of the Magi." "Read the story tonight," she said, "and be prepared to discuss it in class tomorrow." Mrs. Griseldi promised to have the research papers graded and returned no later than Wednesday, following the weekend. The students would have to wait nine days.

No, Mrs. Griseldi wasn't nearly as much fun as Mrs. Anderson, but the class discussions were lively. Alex thought Della was really stupid to sell her beautiful long hair and James was way more stupid to sell his grandfather's gold watch. What a terrible Christmas! James now had a useless gold chain from Della; he'd probably never be able to afford to buy back his watch. And Della now had a pair of beautiful combs to hold up her long hair, which now was ugly and short! James probably hated the way his wife looked. Alex said he thought O. Henry was trying to show how stupid young people can be.

That got Gretchen going! She said "The Gift of the Magi" was the most beautiful story she had ever read. The story wasn't about being smart or stupid; it was about love. Jim loved Della so much that he sold his only valuable possession, something he cherished, his grandfather's watch. Della loved her husband so much that she cut off her beautiful, lustrous hair, sacrificed to give Jim a special gift. "When they're as old as our parents," Gretchen said, "they'll still remember that very special Christmas." (Tryg vowed to find out what his parents thought of the story). After a long and lively debate, nothing resolved, Mrs. Griseldi handed out her version of vocabulary building: ten words from the short story. There would be a test on them tomorrow. English class met during period five. It was Mrs. Griseldi's last class, so she could leave school before the last class of the day, period six. For Tryg, that meant study hall where he reviewed the list:

Imputation
Parsimony
Mendicancy
Depreciate
Meretricious
Scrutiny
Inconsequential
Hysterical
Magi
Instigates

Tryg found each word in the story, then looked up the dictionary definition, making sure he understood each one.

The week passed with agonizing slowness. Even the Saturday matinee, Flash Gordon's ship crashing on a mountainside, failed to distract Tryg's preoccupation with the slow days. Finally, it was Wednesday. The teacher waited nearly the entire 55 minutes before handing out the research papers. Just before the bell rang, Mrs. Griseldi handed the final paper to Tryg and made an announcement.

"I'm very sorry to say that I have to give Mr. Lindstrom an F for his paper. He obviously copied most of what he wrote. He plagiarized. He cheated. Copying someone else's work and turning it in as your own is a kind of lie. Let this be a lesson for all of you."

The class was silent. The bell rang. Tryg was the first to stand, holding his paper, marching out of the classroom, straight to the principal's office. As students passed by in the hallway, Tryg stood in front of the secretary's desk. She smiled and asked Tryg if he needed something. "I'd like to talk to the principal, please. It's important. It's personal. My name is Tryg Lindstrom. I'm a freshman."

"Hello, Tryg," the secretary responded, smiling. "You must be Doc Lindstrom's younger son. Nicholas graduated a couple of years ago. Valedictorian as I remember."

"Yes," Tryg admitted. "Nicholas always had to get straight As."

"Let me see if the principal is free to see you."

A moment later, Mr. Farley opened his door and invited Tryg into his office.

"Welcome to Libby High School," he said. At 13 you're the youngest student we've ever had. I hope you'll be happy here. Please sit down. How can I help you?"

Tryg was calm, composed. He handed his paper to Mr. Farley, showing him the F on the top of the page, and a few lines from Mrs. Griseldi about plagiarism. "Mrs. Griseldi said some bad things about me in class today. That I cheated. That my paper is a lie. She wrote that I had to copy the paragraph on *Sclerophon cementarius* (the scientific name of a mud dauber wasp) from some book, proving that I plagiarized. I'd like for you and me to meet with her--I'd like a chance to defend myself."

Mr. Farley smiled. Across from his desk sat a 13-year-old boy. He should have been frightened, or perhaps furious, or in tears. Instead, the young Lindstrom sat as comfortably as if he had just called for a family meeting. "Mr. Farley," Tryg continued. Wednesday, today, is my father's day off. Sometimes he goes fishing, but today I think he's home. He promised to pick the last raspberries of the year for mother and also take our basset for a walk. I'd like to call home and ask for Father to join us."

Mr. Farley thought for a moment. "Here's what I want you to do,

Mr. Lindstrom. Call your father. Then go to study hall. I'll ask Mrs. Griseldi to come to my office and in a while, I'll ask a hall monitor to find you in study hall for our meeting. Get a hall pass from my secretary for arriving late."

Tryg made his phone call and found a seat in the large open room of desks, a teacher monitoring the room. Students could sit together and talk quietly. Sometimes a "student tutor," was on hand to provide help. A dozen students turned to stare at Tryg; word of his troubles had already circulated. Tryg started working on his algebra homework; maybe he wouldn't have to carry the book home.

A girl with a "Hall Monitor" badge found Tryg. She simply said, "The principal's ready to see you." Tryg got up, a dozen students watching him gather his things. This time the principal's office door was open with three additional chairs in the office. Mrs. Griseldi was already seated. Conrad, towering over the others, held a couple of wooden boxes. Mr. Farley stood behind his desk. Another man was in the room. "Please sit down, everyone," Mr. Farley said. "Let me make some introductions. First, I'd like you all to meet Dr. Stephan Cole, superintendent of Lincoln County schools. He lives just a few houses away and agreed on very short notice to join us." Dr. Cole nodded. "This is Mrs. Griseldi. She has taken over Mrs. Anderson's classes. Dr. Lindstrom is Trygve Lindstrom's father. Trygve especially asked if his father could be here. Trygve has asked for a hearing. He claims that he knows quite a few insects by their scientific names and that he footnoted the only three paragraphs he quoted in his rather long paper."

The room was silent, each person digesting thoughts and emotions. Tryg and Conrad smiled at each other. They looked completely relaxed. Mrs. Griseldi looked uncomfortable, facing the student's father, the school principal and the superintendent of schools. She had not anticipated this kind of confrontation. Mr. Farley continued, "Dr. Lindstrom gave me an idea. He said that if his son could name, say, ten insects by their scientific names and describe them, that Mrs. Griseldi might be willing to acknowledge her . . . shall we say, *misjudgment*. If, however, Trygve's unable to demonstrate his proficiency, he'll be suspended for the next six-week term and have to complete all his schoolwork at home under parental supervision.

Mrs. Griseldi allowed herself a smile. She felt confident she had done the right thing. The boy had plagiarized. This would be a hard but valuable lesson.

"Are you ready, Trygve?" asked the principal.

Tryg stood up. "Yes, sir." He replied simply. "I asked my father to bring a couple of cases with some of my favorite insects." Tryg lifted the largest case from his father's lap. "This beautiful huge moth comes from Madagascar. It's called the moon moth."

"Excuse me, Mr. Lindstrom," Mrs. Griseldi interrupted. "Moon moth is not a scientific name."

Undaunted, Tryg continued. "Of course, you're right, Mrs. Griseldi. His scientific name is *Argema mittrei*. I bought it from a company in Brooklyn. My brother Nicholas set it for me: he's really good at delicate things. You can tell it's a male because the bipectinated antennae are really wide. See, they look like little feathers. The female's antennae are narrow. The female is even bigger, but her tails are not so long and elegant. Father asked one of his patients to make this nice box for me with a glass cover. All I had was a Riker mount." Tryg carefully set the case on an empty chair and lifted the smaller wooden cigar box. "Here are two moths I hatched out myself after I found the cocoons. They're the biggest moths we have in Montana. The first one, with the crescent moon on his wings is *Samia cecropia*. The other is *Telea polyphemus*. See the little window in its wing that looks like an eye. The moth's named after the mythical giant Polyphemus who had only one eye. You can tell this polyphemus is female--see the narrow, feathery antennae? I think the most beautiful moth in the United States is *Actias luna*, a beautiful green moth with tails. Unfortunately, we don't have luna moths in Montana. These moths I'm showing you are all called silk moths, family Saturnidae; their cocoons are made from silk."

Mrs, Griseldi lost her faint smile. She was no longer leaning back in her chair, arms folded, trying to look relaxed. This meeting wasn't turning out to be fun at all. The young boy was actually teaching a class of adults. What had she done? She found it hard to hear the boy's presentation as guilt enveloped her.

"Someday, I'll go to Madagascar," Tryg continued. Ninety percent of the plants and animals are unique to that island. When Father and I visited the Smithsonian, we held hissing cockroaches from Madagascar. They're about, oh, seven centimeters long. When they're disturbed, they rear up and hiss like a snake, but they're harmless, kinds cute--and they make good pets. Oh yeah, their name is *Gromphadorhina portentosa*. The first name means something like "pig nose." There's a beautiful day-flying moth in Madagascar called the sunset moth because of the pink and orange color under its wings. I had one in my collection, but I broke off the wings. Oh yeah, it's called *Urania riphaeus*.

"Most of the insects I know by name are in my animal encyclopedia, including four whole books on insects, or in my very favorite book, *The Butterfly Book* by Holland. The librarian at the county library lets me keep it all summer. My favorite butterflies are swallowtails. *Papilio rutulus* is the western tiger swallowtail. I've got a perfect one in a wooden cigar box. There's another swallowtail I've been trying to catch with three tails on each hind wing called *Papilio multicaudata* which means 'many tails.' Of course, there are some really famous butterflies like the monarch, *Danaus plexippus*, and the painted lady (*Vanessa cardui*). Everyone knows the monarch migrates each year from Canada to Mexico, but the painted lady variety that lives in Europe takes an even longer journey all the way from Africa. I guess everyone knows a honeybee is *Apis mellifera* and a housefly is *Mosca domesticus*. I have a red bodied dragonfly that I watched hatch from our dock on Lake McGregor. Its name is *Libulella saturata*. Most of the insects I collect aren't in my field guide, so I just make up names. I've got a big cricket I just call my "thumb cricket."

"One of my favorite scientific names is for a little red wasp: *Dasmutilla satanis*. She's called a velvet ant, but she's actually a wingless wasp. Her sting is so terrible, someone named her after Satan. Her common name is 'cow killer.'

"Thanks to *National Geographic* I know the names of a few really huge beetles like *Titanus giganteus, Dynastes hercules* and *Acrocinus longimanus*. Someday I'll have these giant beetles in my collection. The most famous beetle is probably the Egyptian scarab, *Scarabeus sacer*. It's a kind of dung beetle. I guess the most important moth in the world has to be the silkworm moth, *Bombyx mori*. It's a small, plain old gray moth, but it supplies the world with silk."

"Thank you, Trygve," Mr. Farley interrupted. "I think you've named about 18 insects and could probably keep talking all night. You can go home, now. Mrs. Griseldi, I'd like you to please stay a bit longer; Mr. Cole and I would like to talk to you."

Suddenly the meeting was interrupted by urgent knocking at the door: enter Mr. Anderson's secretary. "Sorry to disturb your meeting, Mr. Farley, but Dr. Lindstrom is wanted at the hospital. Seems Mrs. Anderson's in labor."

16

The Ice Tunnel
(Tryg, age 15)

Hurt no living thing;
Ladybird, nor butterfly,
Nor moth with dusty wing,
Nor cricket chirping cheerily,
No grasshopper so light of leap,
Nor dancing gnat, nor beetle fat,
Nor harmless worms that creep.

Cristina Rossetti
"Hurt No Living Thing"

The most important function of a high school? Ask a teacher, principal, school board member or superintendent of schools and the unwavering answer will be something like "providing a quality education to the students," or "helping students realize their potential." We've all heard the sentiment. School is about learning, about academics, preparing young minds for success, right? Don't believe it. The number one and number two priorities of our high school: varsity basketball and varsity football (not necessarily in that order). The high school football coach earned more than any teacher, even more than the principal. There was never an assembly for students who made the Dean's List. But every Thursday before a basketball or football game the entire student body filled the gym for a pep rally. Sixth period ended. Teachers stopped teaching. We all filed down the stairs and hallways to the gym. The band played. Cheerleaders sang:

You've got to be a football hero
To get along with the beautiful girls.

Following several rousing, pom pom-shaking cheers, the players gathered on the gym floor wearing handsome wool blue and gold letter jackets, the ones with tan leather sleeves. Then the coach gave his pep talk: how proud he was of his "boys" who were progressing through yet another undefeated season. The coach, by the way, was the consensus worst teacher in our school. He "taught" history by reading from the textbook for a while and then sitting at his desk while we finished the chapter silently in class, answering the questions at the end. If we finished our answers in time, we could turn them in and avoid homework. Football players always turned in their answers by the end of class. So much for the quality education argument.

Sing in the school choir? Don't expect speeches. Write the weekly school newsletter? You won't even get an additional photo in the annual. Serve on student council, belong to the chess club? No letter jacket. The class president was always a basketball or football hero who already had his jacket. No one buys a jacket unless it has a great big "A" on it, for "athlete." Pinned to the letter: badges of honor; silver pins shaped like football pins or basketballs. Our best senior athletes had four of each. Why couldn't they have a pin for good students, maybe something that looked like a brain? And what about the cheerleaders? Pretty sure they would have loved to wear a letter jacket.

High school games took place Friday nights. The football stadium or the gym was always sold out, packed with students and adults. Students got in free with an ID card and sat in the student section next to the band. The visiting team had their reserved section on the opposite side. Adults paid a dollar (kids under 12 free). A box of popcorn cost 25 cents, (profits to the athletic department, of course) but it wasn't the fresh hot buttered kind you get at the movie theater. Home games were even broadcast on our local radio station. When you drive into Libby from either direction on Highway 2, you can't miss the painted wooden sign:

Welcome to Libby
City of Eagles
Proud Home of the Libby Loggers

"Proud Home of Libby Loggers" didn't mean proud of students on the Dean's List. It didn't proud home of the choir or the band or the chess club. Libby Loggers meant our basketball and football team.

During basketball and football season, every other Friday was an away game. Two buses lined up in front of the high school on Friday afternoon for the trip to a rival town: places like Polson or Whitefish, Bigfork or Bonners Ferry. The first bus was for players and coaches and equipment, the second for our six cheerleaders and the 60 students who signed up and paid the $5 bus fee. I didn't miss a single away game.

The bus rides themselves were fun. We played cards. We talked about our teachers. Tony told dirty jokes. We sang all kinds of silly songs:

Old Uncle Mort
He was sawed off and short
He was only five foot two.
But he walked like a giant
When he pulled out a pint (bad rhyme, that)
Of that good ol' mountain dew.

Refrain:

Give me that good old mountain dew,
Them that refuse it are few (mighty few).
I'll hush up my mug if you'll fill up my jug
With that good old mountain dew.

When the bus finally reached our destination, we always rolled down the windows and sang as loud as we could:

John Jacob Jingleheimer Schmidt.
That's my name too.
Whenever we go out,
The people always shout,
John Jacob Jingleheimer Schmidt
La, la, la, la, la, la, la.

The logic of this revered practice is buried in obscurity.

My most vivid memory is a bitter cold trip to Polson. We arrived in town around six p.m., giving us an hour to eat dinner before the game. We piled into the local diner for hamburgers and a coke or a malt. A few brought a sack or lunchbox; they sat with us and mooched French fries. A few took turns playing pinball machines. Then we all walked together like a flock of flamingoes to the gym. Outside, the temp was dropping. By 10 p.m. our victorious team and students hurried onto the buses and settled down for the trip back to Libby. None of the players showered after away games, so we managed to start our return trip with little delay. The snow had stopped; the sky was now clearing, resulting in an arctic temperature of -38 F degrees.

The bus was COLD. Of course, we all had warm coats and gloves, scarves and wool caps. The cheerleaders, still in uniform, wore jeans over tights. But we still shivered; everyone was glad to have a partner to sit next to, closely, for a bit of warmth. Seniors always sat in the back of bus, a dumb, dumb, dumb tradition, because the only heater was at the very front. I found a seat, next to the cold wall and window, waiting for someone to sit next to me. For some reason, Zeke had chosen a different seat for the return trip. Usually, I sat with Alex or Otto, but neither one had signed up for this trip. Most of the seats were filled when Gretchen walked down the aisle and asked if she could sit by me.

Gretchen! A cheer leader! Not just *a* cheerleader, *the head* cheerleader! Gretchen of the blond pigtails and deep blue eyes. Gretchen of the perfect splits and backflips. Gretchen who always looked so happy every minute of every game in her cheerleader skirt, waving pop poms or twirling a baton. Gretchen, an 18-year-old senior, sitting next to a 15-year-old guy? Of course, Gretchen had a boyfriend. Of course, he was the football hero, our quarterback *and* class president. No gossip could possibly emerge from her sitting next to the scrawny 15-year-old.

Still. How good it felt, sitting next to *the* cheerleader. Several guys must have been miserable with jealousy.

The bus began the slow three-hour ride on snowy roads. After our bus driver regaled us with a couple of yodeling songs, and our ineffective demands for "more heat!" we settled down for a long cold ride, most students falling asleep. The bus held 66 students, 67 people counting the bus driver, all puffing clouds of steam. The entire heat supply of the bus struggled just to keep the windshield clear. Within half an hour, all the side windows were frosted. The frost was so thick on the back windows, we could scratch messages or create works of art. I carved a nice longhorn beetle, sure to impress Gretchen. Gradually, the entire bus was transformed into a magical ice tunnel as frost accumulated on walls and ceiling.

Gretchen talked to me! She told me that after the pep rally on Thursday, she had given Jimmie, the football hero, back his class ring. She'd been wearing his class ring around her neck, official emblem of going steady. They had argued about her wanting to be a pediatrician. Everyone knows the man's the boss of the family, he had said, and any wife of his was going to stay home to raise the kids. A mother's place is in the home. She laughed! "He's not the man for me," she said. "I have no idea if there *is* a man for me, but I'm going to be a pediatrician and, God willing, I'm going to have a bunch of kids."

"Maybe you need a house husband," I said. "Or a nanny. For what it's worth, I think you can be anything you want to be: pediatrician *and* mother *and* deep-sea diver *and* circus clown, if you're so inclined, *with* a bunch of kids. *If* you don't marry Jimmie, of course" I added. She laughed and actually squeezed my hand, well, her mitten squeezed my glove, but it still counted.

We had been in several classes together, biology, algebra, trig, two years of English and two years of Latin. (Yes, we actually had classes in Latin in our little high school.) But we had never actually spoken to each other, never sat together in the cafeteria. I suppose this was the very first time I had ever had an actual conversation with a girl. She asked questions about me. What does an entomologist do? I told her that some worked for the government, developing insecticides. That was *not* a job for me. And for sure I wasn't going to be a curator like the one I met at the Smithsonian. Maybe I would teach college kids, if I could find a university with entomology classes. Sorry, I was *not* going to be a house husband. (I was enjoying her laughter and relieved that she had "broken up" with Jimmie without an emotional display. I hate it when people cry.). Maybe I could get a job at National Geographic and go to Africa or to the Amazon and collect big bugs. I found out her dad worked at the vermiculite mine and her mother owned the knitting store on Mineral. My father had delivered her little brother at St. John's Hospital in town. We just talked. It was a strange experience for me, talking to a girl. She said she'd been accepted to college with a scholarship as a cheerleader. She was going to be a pre-med major. I said that's what all the college cheerleaders probably did, majored in pre-med or maybe engineering.

I talked about our lazy basset who had once snagged a roast off the kitchen table and had eaten the whole thing. (We ate at A&W that night.) I told her about my annoying brother. She talked about her father who had emphysema. We wondered why so many miners had lung problems. I told her about my father's coughing which was getting worse. Finally, Morpheus waved his wand over Gretchen. Before she fell asleep, I promised I'd be at her graduation when she got her MD if she (and all of her kids) came to my PhD in entomology ceremony. (Is there a PhD in entomology?) Gretchen fell asleep, her pigtailed head on my shoulder. Painful cold penetrated my arm and shoulder that rested next to the outside wall of the bus. Icy fingers burrowed through my coat and sweater, but I couldn't move and risk waking up my sleeping beauty. I was too uncomfortable to fall asleep. A few people were still talking, some playing a card game in the diffused orange light that managed to shine dimly through the ice-covered ceiling lights. At long, long last I saw the "Welcome to Libby" sign. We passed the lumber mill, turned into the high school parking lot, everyone gasping as they woke up to the wonder of our ice tunnel.

Gretchen got up, eyes half closed against the sudden glare of light. She joined the line of sleepy travelers without saying a word. Now it was my turn to get up, but the left sleeve of my coat was frozen to the wall and window. After a struggle, I pulled my arm free with a loud crack of ice that clung to my coat, a memento of my trip. At least the sleeve was still intact. I was sorry to watch the ice melt after I returned home.

17

Kingfisher Creek
(Tryg, 16)

All things counter, original, spare, strange;
Whatever is fickle, freckled (who knows how?)
With swift, slow, sweet, sour; adazzle, dim;
He fathers-forth whose beauty is past change:
Praise Him.

Gerard Manley Hopkins
"Pied Beauty"

Beauty breaks in everywhere.

Ralph Waldo Emerson

Late in August, Tryg turned 16, that special age when boys faced The Libby Challenge, the portal to manhood: spending the night at Kingfisher Creek. Tryg would have enjoyed going with The Five Rangers, but his four companions had already passed the manhood test two years earlier, when Tryg had been too young to join them. Besides, he was happy to go alone, deciding to bring a couple of insect jars in hopes he might capture a rare beetle.

Anna fussed over her son's preparations, fixing his lunch pail, checking to see he had a warm jacket and an extra pair of socks. Tryg wouldn't suffer from hunger or hypothermia (Conrad commenting gently that the weather report called for a high of mid-eighties). Tryg put on his backpack and Anna inspected her son, now an inch taller than his mother. She felt something like sorrow intertwined with a mother's pride. In two weeks, her son would be off to college. Her little boy (how had it happened so quickly?) had become a young man. He was starting to shave. When did those strong arms and legs take over her boy's skinny frame? How tall would he be when he came home for Christmas?

"Time to go, son," Conrad announced. "We'll drive you to the trailhead and pick you up at noon tomorrow."

Ten miles west of Libby, Conrad pulled to the side of the road, the unmarked trailhead. Tryg quickly gathered his things and kissed his mother, who was making a heroic effort to stem her tears. Soon the young man disappeared into the dense forest, following the narrow dirt trail.

There was nothing particularly noteworthy about Libby's rite of passage. Almost every boy had spent their lives hunting, fishing and sleeping under the stars. Yet no one could deny the mystical importance of the initiation. Boys returned to Libby changed.

It was a fine, warm August day as Tryg descended for half an hour into an old-growth forest, a small section of Kootenai National Forest, protected from logging. Eventually, Tryg heard Kingfisher Creek, gurgling gently. He had reached the first wonder of the day: the forest of giant cedars and tall ferns. Tryg rested a hand on one of the ancient trees, fully six feet in diameter. He wondered if somehow the tree might be aware of his presence. He looked and listened: silence. No twittering birds no scampering squirrels, no whining flies or mosquitoes. The only sound was the faint gurgling of the creek. The dominant aroma: fresh scent of cedar. The trail was softened with a thick blanket of cedar leaves. Tryg was tempted to simply sit for awhile at the base of a tree, an ancient wonder that must be at least a thousand years old.

"This cedar forest is dark and deep, but I have miles to go before I sleep," he muttered.

Now the trail rose steeply. He soon left the ferns and cedars and dark shadows behind. As he climbed, the air grew steadily warmer. Tryg expected to follow Kingfisher Creek all the way to the waterfall, but the trail left the creek behind and Tryg continued to the second wonder, the mountain of turquoise blue shale. The trail was now open to the clear sky and bright August sun. Tryg stopped to take off his outer shirt and drink deeply from his canteen. The trail traversed the steep hillside. Although the trail was three feet wide, Tryg shuddered reflexively as he looked down the hillside. Uncomfortable with heights, he couldn't help thinking that one false step on the trail might result in a terrifying slide hundreds of feet down jagged shards of shale.

Then he saw it! A lovely bright yellow tiger beetle. A treasure for his collection! He carefully slipped off his backpack and found a jar. The beetle seemed to be prancing on the trail in typical rapid jerky bursts of speed. Tryg approached stealthily, hugging the inside of the trail. With a sudden pounce, Tryg brought the jar down, but the beetle was too fast. Gone! Tryg had decided not to bring a butterfly net and now regretted his decision. Maybe he'd get another chance, he hoped. Tryg had only a single tiger beetle in his collection.

The trail descended the shale mountain and Tryg again hiked comfortably among pine and aspen, watching eagerly for the stream and meadow and waterfall. Then he heard it, a distant rush, like wind rustling leaves. Tryg quickened his step; it must be the waterfall. Suddenly he was there, standing above the place so many had described to him: the ribbon waterfall cascading into the pond, the winding stream dotted with beaver ponds, the logjam where so many had caught a trout for dinner, the deep grass and white-barked aspens. He had arrived at the secluded little Shangri-Las to spend the night and declare himself a man.

Tryg decided to sleep near the pond just far enough away from the waterfall to evade the mist that constantly billowed with shifting rainbows. He unshouldered his backpack, retrieved his lunchpail and sank into the tall grass, leaning against the pack. Anna had packed his favorite, a meat loaf sandwich and three chocolate chip cookies, with semi-sweet chips. Coffee in the thermos surprised him: was this

Anna's message--men drink coffee; hot chocolate was a child's beverage? Another surprise: one of Conrad's bent pipes filled with tobacco. Conrad had recently stopped smoking; even a single puff now triggered a bout of coughing. Did Anna expect Tryg to start? He'd talk to her when he returned.

Although he hadn't captured a single insect for his collection, Tryg felt, what was it . . . yes, he decided, it was complete contentment. He took out his fathers's pipe without lighting the tobacco and inhaled the sweet vanilla scent. He had tried smoking once before, hating the taste.

After lunch, Tryg decided to take a swim in the pond. Knowing he was alone, he scrambled out of his clothes and walked to the edge of the pond. As he stepped into the clear water, he was surprised at the harsh chill; he expected the pond to be much warmer in August. It felt as cold as McGregor Lake, a deep natural lake which never seemed to warm in the summer. He plunged into the icy water and swam rapidly to the waterfall, enjoying the invigorating spray of water falling on his head and shoulders. A few minutes later he raced back to shore; eager to feel the warm sun again. It would be many years before he skinny dipped again.

It was now late afternoon and he had things to do, but he paused to appreciate the *afternoon autumnal sunlight filling the woods with the soft light of a legendary land.* Despite the warm day, the night would be cold. He needed to gather firewood, enough to last the night. and gather enough pine needles for a makeshift mattress. Unless he was willing to face some peer-review ridicule (and hunger pangs), he needed to catch a trout for dinner. He managed to slip his still wet body back into his clothes and assembled the four short pieces of his old bamboo rod. Royal coachman: it was his favorite dry fly. Nicholas always scoffed at Tryg's choice; flies should imitate the current insect hatch, he argued. Nicholas, a master of the fly-fisher's art, had reproduced dozens of local insects: mayflies, midges, gnats, stoneflies, salmonflies and grasshoppers. Yet none of Nicholas' patterns were as lovely, none gave such pleasure, as the royal coachman.

Tryg looked at the clear stream, the several beaver ponds, and finally, the deep pool ahead of the logjam. He decided on the deep pool. The short bamboo rod was perfect for Kingfisher Creek. He dropped the coachman ahead of the logjam and let it drift over the pool. Nothing. He tried again and again with no luck. As long shadows settled over the water, Tryg expected trout to begin feeding, but the waters were quiet. The pond was an unlikely spot, since he had just been swimming there and the fish must be spooked. So, he walked to the next prospect, a beaver pond. There they were: dozens of trout. He could see them swimming in the deep end. Tryg dropped a fly onto the still water and retrieved it in little jerks. Half a dozen fish raced to the surface and Tryg pulled in a ten-inch rainbow--plenty for a meal. He took his fish to the edge of the stream to clean it, using his Tippy-sharpened filet knife, and then returned to his campsite.

Now for firewood: the task was easy. He walked across the meadow to the aspen/pine woods and found dead branches clinging to the trunk near the base of nearly every tree. These broke easily and were wonderfully dry and seasoned. He made three trips, gathering more than he'd need for one night. He'd leave a welcome surplus for the next visitor. The sun was just beginning to drop below the trees when Tryg started his fire. Waiting for a perfect bed of coals, Tryg cooked his fish, a stick inserted through the gills, careful not to drop his prize. A bit of salt and the meal was ready. Tryg watched the sky turn pink and orange, listened to the waterfall and then felt the temperature begin to plummet as the sky grew dark, a full moon bathing the valley in white light, the Milky Way glowing.

Then the third wonder of the day. Tryg settled into his sleeping bag, watching the waterfall illumed by moonlight and staring into the glowing coals when the fogfall appeared. Tryg called it a fogfall for lack of a better word. From the top of the waterfall, dense grey mist began rolling in, tumbling silently down the cliff in silent slow-motion. *Lo he comes with clouds descending.* The fog settled onto the surface of the pond, rolling across the surface, layer of mist merging with layer. Tryg watched, mesmerized, as greyness continued to pour into the valley. Soon cold, damp darkness blanketed Tryg's camp, the moon now but a dim blur of light that finally disappeared altogether. Darkness swallowed the Milky Way, the brightest stars and finally the moon. No longer could he watch the *fire-folk sitting in the air*. Against utter darkness, Tryg's campfire produced a small dome of orange light. He added a new supply of wood.

Tryg remembered another fog and limited visibility when Libby's greatest single storm closed the highway and most of the neighboring schools. But that fog lived in a world of white; this was a fog of utter darkness. Tryg was filled with ineffable joy. The sound of an invisible waterfall. The glow of his campfire and the cold, wet blackness: Tryg felt he must be experiencing something precious, mysterious. He decided to slip out of his sleeping bag, put on his jacket and walk toward the sound of the waterfall, to the edge of the pond. With each step, the glow of the campfire diminished until only a faint dot of orange light remained. If he continued walking, the light would surely disappear, and he would be lost in darkness and cold until morning. Soon his clothes were drenched in the waterfall's spray and the mist of the fog. He returned to camp, the fire glow expanding with each returning step. By the light of his campfire and its welcome warmth, he took out the small notebook he always carried with him and began writing:

The Holiness of Night

Oh Lord, help me to understand
The holiness of night.
Let me embrace, in perfect trust,
The dusk and fading light.

The busy world is hushed and calm,
Thy hidden gifts revealing.
Let me surrender to Thy peace,
Thy sacred time of healing.

The Magi night-watched from afar,
Your star their only guide.
I too endeavor to discern
This darkness you abide.

Oh Lord, accept my serenade,
Embracing darkness, unafraid.

In the morning, Tryg, now officially initiated into manhood, watched the fog lift and reluctantly left his now favorite place. He promised himself he'd return.

18

Jennings Rapids (Tryg, age 18)

Laughter is nothing else but sudden glory arising from some sudden eminence in ourselves.

Thomas Hobbes

At its heyday The K Swenson Lumber Company employed a thousand men. The mill supported a thousand families, helped to pay for a thousand homes and trailers and apartments. Even though more than 100 men worked at the mine, we were a lumber town, our high school mascot: the Libby Loggers. Every weekday, logging trucks rolled into the mill with newly felled cedar, Douglas fir, ponderosa, spruce and lodgepole. Every day, the mill shipped out lumber, wooden boxes, Presto-Logs and telephone poles. After my junior year of undergraduate school, having at last turned 18, I finally got a summer job at the mill working in the pole yard where our usual task was turning logs into telephone poles. My title was "tagger/brander," the entry level job paying $2.35 an hour. My take-home pay was a princely $160 every two weeks. Loggers earned the most money, upwards of $10,000 a year. The average mill worker made $8,000 after five years.

Of course, things cost a lot less back then. Gas was 35 cents a gallon, (30 cents in Kalispell), milk 85 cents a gallon. Our house in Libby cost $12,000. A brand-new Ford or Chevvy was about $1,500. Father's

Jeep cost $2,400, winch included. When mother sent me to the store for a dozen eggs, a loaf of bread and a couple of apples, I got seven cents back from a dollar bill.

My main job was to stamp little metal disks into tags with information like the size of the log (A "9/30" telephone pole meant nine inches in diameter and 30 feet long.) the date and of course the name of our mill. I then drilled a half-inch deep hole about 1.5 inches in diameter in the log at the correct height, slipped in the disk and hammered in a nail. Lowest on the, well, telephone pole, I did other menial tasks like sweeping sawdust off the deck and sharpening chain saw blades, which always reminded me of Tippy. For some reason, we branded only cedar logs, noble giants three or four or even six feet in diameter. I hated the branding, standing over the electric branding iron and breathing in the acrid cedar smoke.

The mill was essential to Libby's economy, but the lumber industry can be a dangerous beast. The box factory, for example, produced wooden boxes, most commonly for shipping fruits and vegetables. Workers wore earplugs to soften the constant high-pitched whining of sawblades. They wore leather gloves that offered virtually no protection against the blur of sharp spinning blades. A mist of sawdust always filled the air; some wore a handkerchief over nose and mouth; others simply tolerated the workplace conditions. No one wore protective goggles. Father dealt with many of the casualties. The work was repetitious and mind-numbing. Small pieces of wood raced through the sawblades, over and over and over. Splinters in the eye were common. One careless, absentminded move could result in a lost thumb or finger.

The most dangerous part of the logging industry took place outside the mill, in the woods where trees were felled, limbs removed, logs dragged to waiting logging trucks, loaded and then delivered. The mill had never lost a lumberjack, but there had been plenty of close calls. The worst accident happened to Ingmar, a terrible crushing blow of a ponderosa log that bounced on other logs and fell from the truck bed. Father was unable to save Ingmar's leg. Swenson himself flew Ingmar to Spokane in his private plane. Three months later Mr. Swenson paid for Ingmar's prosthetic limb. From then on, the man worked in the box factory, sitting on a stool; Swenson kept him on logger wages,

My corner of the mill, the pole yard, had its own set of dangers. The most common hazard, the poles themselves, freshly pulled from the huge pond and stripped of bark, ready to be cut and drilled and tagged. As the logs moved across the two moving chains, (the "pole deck") we often had to climb onto the logs that were dangerously slippery. Falls were common, bruising knees and hips. I fell plenty of times, carrying a peeve, a razor-sharp blade at the end of a wooden handle, used for removing remnants of bark. Each fall elicited laughter and applause from the rest of the crew. I was careful to keep the peeve blade pointed away from my legs and feet. The greatest danger was chainsaws, sometimes two or three operating at the same time, cutting the ends of logs to the proper length. The year before I started working there, Ivan the Terrible backed into the tip of a chainsaw. Father says chainsaw wounds are nasty. The teeth rip chunks of denim and then flesh. Oil and sawdust contaminate the wound. Ivan was rushed to the hospital where Father patched up the wound as best as he could. Two days later, The Terrible was back at work, but he stood at the break table for a month and after that, sat on a small pillow. The next summer, the crew joked and laughed about "Ivan's Butt." Ivan and I didn't laugh.

With the exception of the lowly tagger/brander position, the pole yard crew had been together for years. Since it was the lowest-paying job, people transferred to other jobs as soon as they were posted. I was not only a rookie, but Doc Conrad's boy. When I was hired, Jake, the pole yard foreman made it clear that "college kids" had to prove themselves. There'd be no special treatment for Doc's kid. All I had to do was work hard and do what I was told and I'd get along. Several of my friends had a father or older brother who worked at the mill; they gave me some good advice. Old-timers liked to poke fun at the new guys who showed up wearing new stuff, so:

Whatever you do, don't come to work in a new pair of jeans. Wear your oldest, faded jeans to work.

You have to wear steel-capped boots, so your boots will be brand new. Get them scuffed up and dirty.

Bring an old lunch pail and beat-up thermos.

Wear a T-shirt, definitely not a shirt with buttons.

Every new hire is issued a brand-new hard hat. Pole yard hats are white. Breakrooms have extras, old ones hanging on the wall. Take one of the old ones.

I'd still be a rookie, of course, but at least I didn't need to look like one.

Jake came around every week or so. After half the summer he finally came up to me and said, "You're doing OK, kid." That was it, but I've seldom been more pleased. I remember two things about Jake: his ponderous belly protruded way over his belt and about Jake and his boots were splattered with tobacco juice. He had a round spot on his back pocket where he kept a tin of the stuff. Every once in a while, he'd spit.

I never really became part of the pole yard "gang." After all, I'd be leaving for school again at the end of the summer. I was just a "college kid." The next summer I got the same job at the same pay with the same crew. And I was still a rookie.

At lunchtime in the break shack, four of the men played a few quick hands of poker. They each carried a pocketful of pennies dumping a pile of them on the table. They kept an old deck of cards on the table. One day, Frank actually talked to me. "Hey Kid, (no one called me Tryg), take a look at this." He picked up a grey penny. "Ever seen one of these before?" I looked at the strange penny, dated 1943. "In 1943," he continued, "they needed copper for the war, so they made steel pennies that year. I'll sell it to you for a dime." I didn't know if it was worth a dime, and I didn't care. I had to have that steel penny.

"Could I bring you a dime tomorrow?" I asked, embarrassed to have nothing in my pockets.

"Sure, Kid," he said. I'll save it for you. It's kind of a war souvenir."

I still have that coin, my lumber mill souvenir.

I sat at another table and mostly just listened to the conversations.

Sure is hot today.

Looks like a thunderstorm's coming.

I hear we're getting a rush order--maybe we'll get some Saturday overtime.

Overtime was great. Time-and-a-half meant an extra 28 dollars.

One of the men rolled his own cigarettes. I enjoyed watching the ritual: sprinkling tobacco onto the paper (random flakes falling to the ground), levelling the tobacco and then rolling the paper around the tobacco, licking the last edge of the paper and completing the roll, twisting one end and putting the other end in his mouth (spitting out a few flakes) and finally lighting the cigarette. The break shack was always filled with smoke. Recently, the talk was about Logger Days. Every July the mill closed down for a Thursday, Friday and the weekend for Logger Days. The four-day celebration drew hundreds of loggers from neighboring towns to take part in the celebration. Popular competitions included log rolling, cutting logs with a crosscut saw, an axe and a chain saw, and loading a stack of logs onto the trailer of a logging truck. The stores all advertised "Crazy Days," with bargain prices. Unfortunately, .22 shells still cost the same. A favorite activity was the exhibition of more than 100 restored old cars, all angle-parked on Mineral Ave from Highway 2 down to the railroad tracks. Lovely, shiny classic cars arrived from as far as Spokane and Cour d'Alene. Everyone in town gathered to eat turkey legs and corn on the cob, watch the arm-wrestling contests or stroll by the wonderful old cars. But this year I was impatiently waiting for Sunday.

Sunday, the grand finale of Logger Days, featured a daring float down Jennings Rapids. You won't find the rapids today. When the Army Corps of Engineers built Libby Dam, the rapids disappeared under Lake Koocanusa. But back then, perhaps a hundred boats and rafts lined up five miles upstream from Libby at the launch site. It wasn't easy convincing Mother to let Otto and me take our 12-foot boat on the Kootenai, much less through the rapids. She found it difficult to acknowledge that we were now men. Finally, she relented, insisting we wear our life vests.

How can I describe the Kootenai? It's big and powerful, with pools a jaw-dropping 100 feet deep. The turquoise-colored river begins in the far north of British Columbia in Kootenay National Park. By the time the river reaches Libby, the river flows at ten thousand cubic feet a second in its nearly 500-mile journey. From Bonners Ferry, Idaho, the river flows north again, back into British Columbia into Kootenay Lake eventually joining the Columbia River. Fisherman come for the trout: rainbow, cutthroat, bull and the occasional brown, attracted to two to three thousand trout per mile. In 1997 an angler landed a monster 33-pound rainbow. In the winter, whitefish predominate. White sturgeon, once common, still glide through these deep waters as well as two dozen other species from salmon to catfish. Tell you a secret: try fishing right where the Fisher River joins the Kootenai--people still catch the occasional sturgeon there. Jennings Rapids was rated Class III and IV, but less dangerous than Kootenai Falls, a few miles farther downstream.

Otto and I had a long wait to launch our small boat. Most of the loggers had 16-to-20-foot dories with large outboard motors. Others had large self-bailing rafts rated for the Grand Canyon. But our little boat was wonderfully buoyant, with an inner air pocket. We were young, invincible, naïve. At last, it was our turn to launch. I parked Father's Jeep and trailer a couple of blocks away while Otto held the boat near the shore and then eagerly jogged to join him. We were off!

Otto sat in the middle seat rowing us from the shoreline to deeper waters. Although dozens of boats had launched ahead of us, we spied only a single boat downstream and two recently launched boats upstream. I sat in the back with the 10HP motor, the gas tank in the bow. Both of us wore swim trunks and t-shirts, floppy hats, sport shoes, dark glasses and of course, our bulky orange life vests. We felt terribly self-conscious about the vests. While each person had to have a vest in the boat, very few actually wore them. No one wore a helmet. Otto stopped rowing and we relaxed as we drifted with the current, passing stands of pine and aspen. We dipped our hats in the water and drenched our t-shirts against the sun. Two bold men on the great Kootenai River. Despite our summer tans, Mother had smeared us with sunblock.

The shorelines of dense pine slipped past us. Above, two osprey circled; we hoped to see one dive for a trout. We also hoped to spot bald eagles; Libby's known for its eagles. Very gradually, our pace began to quicken. The shoreline seemed to be picking up speed and our boat began bobbing on river waves. Then we heard it, the sound of rushing water. Downstream the river seemed to be boiling. The waves had become whitecaps and a large boulder loomed ahead. Otto grabbed the oars and guided us safely past the boulder, our small boat responding easily. We looked at the shoreline, now lined with hundreds of people, watching boats entering the rapids.

Suddenly we were rocking, twisting, plummeting into a swell and then leaping up a crest. The oars were useless; we just gripped the sides of the boat to avoid being thrown into the froth. Otto yelled something, but I couldn't hear his words over the crashing turbulence. One time the bow plunged so suddenly and steeply that Otto lost his grip and nearly tumbled overboard. Our confidence was gone. Somehow in the confusion the boat had managed to point itself downstream. If we had turned sideways, I'm sure we would have capsized. Last year's *Libby Logger* reported that 22 boats had capsized. No one had ever drowned on Logger Days, but I was suddenly glad to be wearing a life vest. Another sudden downward plunge and crash! The hull struck a hidden boulder, nearly knocking us to the bottom of the boat. Several inches of water washed against our feet as we whipped around 180 degrees, now sliding downriver stern first. Otto grabbed the oars and turned us around just as another wave lifted us and slapped us down. I saw a look of terror on Otto's face; I'm sure he observed the same emotion in mine.

Then a strange thing happened: we both began laughing. Huge gulps of terrified, exultant, inexplicable laughter. The roller coaster of excitement overwhelmed both of us. We were completely helpless, caught in the fury, the excitement and the danger. We bounced and twisted at the mercy of the river, drenched in river spray, engulfed in river roar. A foot of water surged about our feet, but we couldn't let go of our desperate grip to grab the bailing buckets. Suddenly the turmoil subsided. We realized that Jennings Rapids was behind us! We had conquered the rapids! Well, at least we had survived them. We laughed again. We shouted. This time the laughter was born of triumph and relief. Quickly we began bailing water.

Otto yelled, Hooray!"

I yelled, "*Alium furiosum momentum voluptatis!*"

The river had now narrowed; we were moving swiftly, but without the chaos and noise and jarring and danger. The roar of Jennings Rapids abated. Around the next bend the good old bridge at good old Libby came into view. The bridge was lined with people, waving and cheering. I wondered if our parents might be watching. But there was a problem. Otto noticed it first. "We're sinking!" he yelled. And so we were. It wasn't the half foot of water still in the boat that alarmed us. We were each making good progress with our bailing. But our boat was still edging downward into the river. Our collision with the boulder had punched a hole in our hull and that wonderfully buoyant air pocket was filling with water. Time for the Evenrude. I tipped the outboard into the water and pulled the rope. Oh, what a glorious sound: the engine roared to life, and we began chugging toward the shore. The boat moved sluggishly but managed to propel us closer and closer to the shallows. Otto moved to the center seat as the bow threatened to dive. Water was just a few inches from the gunwales as someone waded out to us and grabbed the bow. I killed the engine and tilted it forward. We managed to drag our poor injured boat onto the bank, bow pointed downhill and watched river water drain out of a baseball-sized hole. Otto and I then walked to the bridge where shuttles took the boaters back to the launch site. With help from onlookers, we managed to lift the boat back on the trailer and drive home.

I didn't know how Father would react, especially when he saw the boat. Mother gave me a huge hug and a withering glance to Father, some secret warning I suppose. Seems the news of our adventure preceded my return and my parents had talked to each other. Father simply smiled and gave me a hug. All he said was, "Anna's made meat loaf."

Turns out the boat could be easily repaired with a fiberglass patch. Over the years my little boat has required a bit of TLC: sanding, varnishing, painting. But it's one of my prized possessions, tied to my dock on the Yaak.

19

The Mouse and the Spider
(Tryg, age 18)

Few if any of the structures built by lower animals are more wonderful than the webs of the orb weaver.

The Spider Book
John Henry Comstock

I don't like spiders. OK, to be perfectly honest, I'm an arachnophobe. I'm both morbidly fascinated and frightened by them. I can watch them for hours, spinning a web, catching prey, mating, (the male often cannibalized by the much larger female). But I keep a safe distance. I watch, fascinated, and yet I shudder. Spider enthusiasts feel compelled to write *apologias* for these creatures. They point out how spiders help keep certain insect populations in check (I question that claim.); how most are timid and harmless to humans. How important spiders are in the grand ecological scheme. What if every spider on earth suddenly disappeared? I'd be happy. I think Mother Earth would get along just fine. These spider people refuse to admit a few facts:

1. Let's be honest: spiders are ugly.
2. Spiders are creepy.
3. Some spiders *are* dangerous to humans.
4. Spiders are creepy.

5. Spider silk's a particularly unpleasant substance.
6. Did I mention spiders are creepy?

I admit to a certain grudging fondness for jumping spiders, when observed from a safe distance of course. One thing in their favor: they're small. Some tropical varieties called peacock spiders are multicolored. They're almost cute. Another point in their favor: they don't build webs. I kind of like their little green or turquoise eyes and the jerky way they flit from stem to leaf. It's exciting to watch a jumping spider hunt an insect, suddenly leaping on a housefly. But if I discovered a jumping spider actually *on* me I'd jump up as if on fire. I start shaking if I have to enter a crawl space, certain that spiders are poised to drop onto me, fangs dripping poison. I'm pretty sure spiders sense my fear and just wait for a chance to startle me, or worse.

This attitude, this admixture of revulsion and fear, I freely admit is beneath the dignity and intellect of a scientist, an aspiring entomologist. I've been stung by bees and wasps, but don't feel the same primal terror of them that spiders evoke. By contrast, I feel a genuine camaraderie, an affection, for any kind of beetle and enjoy something akin to love for elaters (click beetles). I'm quite fond of butterflies and moths, grasshoppers and crickets, dragonflies and cicadas. But keep me from spiders . . . and their cousins, centipedes! You can add earwigs to the list.

One particularly harrowing experience haunts me to this day.

Walking slowly through a Pacific coast forest, trying to find a banana slug, I nearly collided with an enormous web spanning the trail. Just the thought of colliding with a web starts my heart racing. The huge orb web extended fully five feet across the trail between two trees, and from the ground to perhaps seven feet high. What kind of monster spider could have spun such a structure, I wondered, taking an instinctive step backwards. And where was the spider now? What if there was a whole family of them? Lurking, watching me.

Suddenly the web started shaking violently. Something must be trapped in the web and struggling to escape. Then I saw it. A mouse! A little mouse, entangled at the base of the web, jerking, writhing and pawing frantically with all four legs. Then it lay still for a moment, perhaps exhausted from its struggles. I wondered how long the mouse had been there. I marveled that a mouse could be held by a spider web.

Then I saw the spider. Something out of a nightmare. A huge black and gold orb weaver. This was no cute jumping spider. It was more fearsome than a tarantula. The abdomen must have been 2.5 centimeters long, the cephalothorax another two centimeters. And those long legs: at least three centimeters.

The mouse suddenly gyrated again, kicking up a small puff of dust from the trail; the huge spider quickly retreated. When the mouse lay still (I could see it panting), the spider cautiously reapproached. I'm guessing the spider had never captured such a bulky treasure. A large moth or a cicada would provide a generous feast, but could a mouse become a victim?

I took a couple of steps forward, gripped by spider-terror and yet compelled to watch the unfolding drama. The mouse seemed to be tiring, the protesting struggles becoming less violent and of shorter duration. The spider cautiously moved closer and closer, each retreat shorter. I could tell the spider was gaining confidence, preparing some kind of attack. The mouse looked at me, terror in those little eyes, I imagine the little guy was equally terrified of me and of that horrible black and yellow predator.

I had to do something. I took a few steps backward on the trail and found a thin dead branch. Returning to the web, I poked the web just above the furry prisoner. I was shocked at the terrible firm grip of the web. When I pulled the stick back the mouse suddenly bolted away, liberated, trailed by a veil of web. The spider, also startled, raced away, disappearing into the shadows.

I'm not fond of mice. I set traps in the house when I see one. But for some reason I felt an inexplicable moment of happiness. I had saved a mouse from what might have been a horrible fate. I tossed the branch into the web where it stayed firmly suspended in space. I sometimes have awful dreams of spiders, always black and yellow orb weavers.

I hope I never see another.

20

Tennis Anyone? (Tryg, age 18)

First one in.

Joe Nigg

My tennis game, at best, is lame.
Sometimes the racket smites my shin.
I frequently forget the score.
The sun! the wind! They're both to blame,
When a Dunlop sails through the tennis court door.
Was my serve out? Or was it in?
I can hardly wait for our next game.

Tryg Lindstrom

Tryg turned 16 shortly before he entered college. Most of his young life he had been the youngest and the smallest kid in class. He was now the youngest freshman, but he had finally begun to grow. Over the summer he had gained 20 pounds and three inches in height. During his first year, he added 15 more pounds and reached his full stature of six feet, three inches, two inches shorter than his father but two inches taller (to his delight) than his brother. Finally, at least physically, Tryg fit in! One requirement for all first-year students was a year of physical education. So many choices! He considered weightlifting, swimming, archery, golf, baseball and tennis. Golf, that would be something he could play all his life. But spending at least four hours to play 18 holes-- too much. And golf required a substantial investment: clubs, bag, golf balls. When he visited The Sports Emporium a few blocks from campus, he spotted a Tad Davis wooden racket with beautiful laminations. It reminded him of the Morley canoes he had admired when fishing at Seeley Lake. Whenever anyone asked him why he had chosen to play tennis, he admitted he had been unable to resist the beauty of a tennis racket.

Tryg had never hit yet a tennis ball. He had never stepped onto a tennis court. But he had played ping pong for years with his father and older brother. How different could it be? He had new tennis shoes and shorts and a polo shirt, just like the others. He *looked* like a tennis player. He lined up with the others and when it was his turn, tossed the ball in the air and took a mighty swing. He struck the ball on the very top of the racket frame, the ball hopping a few feet straight up and bouncing, mockingly, at his feet. Muffled titters. At the end of that first practice, the coach took him aside, after which Tryg went out at dawn every day that fall, (quite a sacrifice for someone who scheduled his earliest class at 10 so he could sleep in). Tryg was teaching himself to serve. In the winter, the tennis class moved indoors. There were only four indoor courts, so everyone played doubles. Tryg was the worst player. Then he was one of the worst. Then he was passable, with an improving serve and fast on his feet. But he quickly excelled at the net, where his ping pong skills transferred to quick reflexes. By spring quarter, the coach invited him to join the freshman team.

Two years later, Tryg was the best player on the tennis team, a ranked Division II college player. He displayed an unusual variety of backspin, topspin and sidespin shots that baffled opponents. His greatest weapon had become the serve, one the scouts described as "heavy." Tryg began experiencing something entirely new that year: popularity. As the usually mediocre tennis team began moving up in the ranks, students began filling the stands. Tryg began winning matches. A few students even asked for his autograph! But there was a fly in the ointment: Coach Carter. Carter yelled at the players. The better the team played, the higher the team rose in league standings, the more aggressive and abusive Coach Carter became. Some of the players laughed at "Old Yeller" behind his back, but Tryg took the insults to heart, whether directed at him or his teammates.

The next Saturday, the team now ranked number two in then conference played its longtime nemesis. The tournament would determine final rankings. Coach Carter gathered his players together and delivered his most volatile, dramatic speech, recorded by the local television station. The opponents were "The Enemy." Coach Carter demanded that The Enemy be defeated, crushed, humiliated. The stands were full. The matches were being televised. The men's doubles team lost. The women's doubles team won. Then the women's singles player emerged victorious in a hard-fought match. One match left: the men's singles. If Tryg won his match, his team would be number one! If he lost, the tournament would end in a tie, but they'd end the season ranked second.

Tryg won the first set in a tiebreaker. The home crowd was ecstatic. The second set was a bit easier, Tryg breaking his opponent's serve and winning 6 - 3. Then Tryg began coughing. The doctor at the college clinic had diagnosed him with asthma, but the symptoms were infrequent. Tryg asked for a time out and retrieved his rescue inhaler. At least he seemed to be breathing normally. One more set and Tryg could lift the crystal trophy. Tryg took a second puff and returned to the court, the crowd strangely hushed.

That's when Coach Carter began yelling. Tryg was embarrassed, then disgusted. He was ashamed of his coach. When his opponent hit a weak defensive lob. Carter shouted, "Kill it!" Tryg tapped the lob at a sharp angle, easily winning the point. Carter screamed, "What the hell are you doing, Lindstrom? Crush the bastard!" Someone from the university escorted the coach from courtside.

Despite struggling for breath after a long rally, Tryg won his match in straight sets. He held the trophy; people took his picture.

Then he quietly resigned from the team. He left a note on the coach's desk: *I do desire to become better strangers.* Competitive tennis was no longer fun. He saved his beautiful wood racket long after aluminum and then composite rackets appeared. From then on, he played tennis with friends, for fun, for fellowship and a congenial cappuccino afterwards.

21

Muerte Canyon
(Tryg, age 27)

*Oh, I have slipped the surly bonds of Earth
And danced the skies on laughter-silvered wings.*

John Gillespie Magee
"High Flight"

I have no fear of the future. Let us go forward into its mysteries.

Winston Churchill

The narrow basalt walls of Muerte Canyon drop 600 feet into the churning white water of Shadow River. Throughout the year, the river plunges through the canyon in perpetual darkness, except for a few spectacular seconds, on a single day in early spring and for the same few seconds on a single day in late autumn, when a shaft of sunlight aligns perfectly all the way down the narrow canyon walls to the river which suddenly bursts into dazzling light. Permission to access is rarely granted to non-native visitors, as the site on the Blackfeet Reservation is considered sacred by the Crow, Kootenai and Blackfeet tribes.

Christian Damberger
Hidden Wonders

After five hours of steady hiking Conrad was beginning to get nervous. He unbuckled his waist strap and let the backpack slide to the ground, draining his last water bottle. No reason to ration: water wasn't going to be a problem. He should soon be at the rim of the canyon of the Shadow River. But would he arrive in time? He had only 45 minutes and was still looking ahead eagerly for the western rim. His lungs burned with each step. His plan had been to take 20 paces and then rest until panting subsided. But his stops grew longer, interrupted by a racking cough, his phlegm spotted with blood. Could he have mistakenly taken a side trail? Would his labor be in vain? He slipped off his new bright red hoodie, emblazoned with the blue and white Norwegian cross, fished out a Bit-o-Honey (Tryg's contribution to the backpack) and savored the confection. Then he re-shouldered the modest burden, resolved by sheer will to increase his pace.

He couldn't have started his pilgrimage much earlier. In the early morning darkness from base camp, he had mechanically unzipped his sleeping bag, emerging from the small frost-covered nylon tent to be greeted by a sliver of crescent moon and a grand display of fire folk. He lit the burner on the compact white gas stove to make a mug of strong chicory coffee, gingerly sipping from his favorite blue enameled tin cup, letting the steam warm his face. Before falling asleep that night he had sipped the single malt from the flask Nicholas had packed and reread Anna's letter and Tryg's poem. He was alone; not another human being within a 10-mile radius. Three difficult river crossings had virtually assured his complete seclusion. Later in the season rivers would be easy to ford and a few other hikers able to gain tribal approval might venture into this sparsely traveled corner.

By the first glow of dawn that morning, he had downed the last bites of scrambled eggs and Canadian bacon, drained his metal mug and slipped on the battered backpack. Didn't come across packs like this one anymore: supple oiled leather nearly black with age, exterior wooden frame. One of the closure straps was missing and the embossed Norwegian flag had finally melted away. Despite the comfort of steaming eggs, melted cheese, bacon and coffee, he felt chilled as he prepared for his trek. Heavy fog still hovered close to the ground and the trail was slippery with frost clinging to the grass. He said farewell to his camp, leaving tent, sleeping bag, mug and camp stove behind. The sign ahead read, "Blackfeet Reservation. Entrance Strictly forbidden Without Council Approval."

With another puff on his rescue inhaler, inhaling as deeply as he could, Conrad had set a steady pace and had fallen into a comfortable, familiar rhythm he prayed he could maintain for the final ascent. He had prepared for this hike for months, hiking his beloved Cascades, trying to build a bit more stamina. But pain had been gaining traction on his battered lungs.

For years Father had spoken of this place with a strange, hushed voice, a kind of reverence. We'd hiked hundreds of trails, but he refused to take me to Muerte Canyon.

"Except for the First Nations, only a handful of people have ever seen this canyon," Father had often said. "It's a journey each person has to take alone."

Within an hour he had climbed above the pockets of fog that now shone like snow patches below. He slipped on dark glasses against the brilliant glare of the early morning sun. His breath puffed out rhythmic clouds of steam into the chill air. Conrad gradually forgot about the weight of the modest pack and relaxed in the tranquility of pristine mountain forest: the chatter of a squirrel, the raucous crowing of ravens, the curiosity of a young deer. He took mental notes of golden fungus on a dead tree trunk, an occasional patch of snow in deep shadows, last season's rose hips clinging to a wild rose bush. Every detail seemed important. A large ground beetle crossed the path; Conrad smiled remembering that young Tryg had called them Mortuary Beetles, always dressed in black. It was far too early for wildflowers or for a hatch of biting flies that can torment a hiker, especially in the spring. He welcomed the warming sun, streaming over the crest of soaring, pink-frosted mountain peaks. For the next hours he hiked, twenty paces and a short stop; twenty more paces, cursing the moments of coughing. He was wheezing now with every breath, munching on bits of venison jerky and sipping water. His pace grew slower, his stops longer. Time for the last of his pain meds. He swallowed the last three. He knew he had to hurry, no matter the physical cost.

With immense relief, he realized that the incline was finally levelling off. He must be near the summit. In a few minutes the trail, the woods, the vegetation suddenly ended at an expanse of dark gray rock. The rim! He could see the expanse of black basalt ahead. Conrad, lone intruder in a secret, sacred land, had found the summit of Muerte Canyon. In the distance, an owl called his name.

Still a few hundred feet from the near wall of the canyon, he could hear the distant, menacing sibilance of rushing water. Six hundred feet below him the Shadow River snarled and boiled. Once Conrad had ventured up the river and into the start of the canyon, clinging to the narrow trail, nearly overwhelmed by the blinding spray and deafening roar, thrilled at the sheer violence of cascading water, a writhing serpent of bellyaching, raging, chastening, hastening, evil-grinning, spinning, bombastic, whirlpool-tumbling, swirling, rock-crushing fury. He had looked up the canyon walls at the narrow ribbon of bright blue sky. Now, from this lofty perch, the river's violence far below had diminished to a persistent distant reptilian *hissssss*.

Conrad set down his pack on a patch of dry grass and listened. He was afraid. Afraid to move closer. Conrad had always felt a terror of heights. He imagined the rocks giving way and casting him into the abyss. Afraid to look down, down, down the narrow canyon walls. Afraid to venture past the familiar comfort of trees and kinnikinnick. The sudden change of landscape was unsettling; he felt like an intruder. He stood, taking small timid steps, ashamed of his timidity, confronting the dreadful irony of his fear. But he still had plenty of time to prepare himself.

Conrad opened his backpack and removed the lunchbox and thermos Anna had prepared. Of course, it was his favorite: a meatloaf sandwich with his favorite honey mustard, cinnamon roll and a thermos of now tepid cocoa. A Clark's nuthatch eyed the backpack hoping for a promising morsel.

Conrad had arrived in time. The sun was directly overhead, rays slowly creeping down the sheer gray walls. He forced himself to walk to the edge and stare into the dark abyss. In a few minutes a flash of light would illumine the white water below. He watched the mocking ravens below him, skillfully soaring the thermals; a two-inch gray lizard that stared into his eyes. Oh, how he hated his fear of heights. The bright sunshine and impossibly blue sky offered no comfort, no warmth or cheer. Something ominous hung in the air like a cold, wet velvet blanket. He understood the fear of ancient sailors, loath to approach the edge of the ocean. With each step, he could see farther down those sheer canyon walls. He sank to all fours and moved like an animal, closer and closer to the edge, wincing as the rocks clawed at his kneecaps. Oh, to be a lizard or an eagle.

He clasps the crag with crooked hands.

Across the cruel narrow canyon, shadowed black columns of basalt plunged down, down to the river. Conrad fought fear and vertigo and giddy exhilaration; the river, like the owl, whispered his name. As he neared the edge, he lay on his belly inching forward, forcing his head over the edge. Down, down, down he looked at the shadows, listened to the rumbling, roiling waters beneath impenetrable, utter consuming blackness.

> *A Dungeon horrible, on all sides round . . .*
> *No light, but rather darkness visible*
> *Serv'd only to discover sights of woe,*
> *Regions of sorrow, doleful shades, where peace*
> *And rest can never dwell, hope never comes*

Misty air rushed up the basalt cliffs, driving a frigid spike of pain into his forehead. He began trembling. Was the very ground itself rumbling underneath him? Below him two black pairs of wings soared in patient circles. Ospreys? Eagles? Vultures? He shivered.

Down, down, down the lichen-encrusted basalt sentinels a band of sunlight continued to creep lower and lower, turning the ancient black columns to deathly gray, spectral ruins of some monstrous pipe organ. The sun was nearly perfectly overhead, fingers of light insinuating, daring, probing, intruding ever farther down the cliffs. This was the moment Conrad had been waiting for. He waited, immersed in the auditory fury of cascading spray and roar of a river that for a thousand millennia had torn bark from fallen trees and relentlessly carved new layers of bedrock. Lower, lower, the sun crept down both cliff faces, *darkness scattering into flight*, illuminating a dozen dancing rainbows in the boiling, swirling mists, while the river, still plunged in shadow, hissed with malevolent, mocking intensity.

As the Light of Light descendeth
From the realms of endless day,
That the powers of hell may vanish
As the darkness clears away.

Foot by patient foot, sunlight crept ever deeper into the abyss, farther and farther down the canyon walls reaching for the boulder-strewn riverbed.

Flash!

Sunlight, perfectly aligned above the canyon, burst in full glory onto the river. Like a twisted neon light, the river spume exploded into dazzling whiteness, a bolt of liquid lightning, both sides of the canyon now flung into black shadow. Past and future--too bright! Conrad shielded his eyes; he heard an alleluia chorus.

And then, just as suddenly, the flash expired. The show was over. The long fingers of the sun's rays began re-ascending the walls, the river again engulfed in shadow. One by one, the dancing rainbows disappeared, basalt sentinels reverting to black. Conrad stood, gasping for breath, shaky and nauseous.

Then came his laughter, his full-voiced hearty laughter, the sheer exhilaration, the joy, the tears. "*Alium furiosum momentum voluptatis,*" he shouted. His fear had evaporated. *I will fear no evil.*

He stepped forward.

And like a thunderbolt, he falls.

22

Last Rites
(Tryg, age 27)

We are molded and remolded by those who have loved us. . . . No love, no friendship can ever cross the path of our destiny without leaving some mark upon it forever.

Francois Mauriac

Three days after Dr. Lindstrom was reported missing, a park ranger discovered a body on the banks of the Shadow River. He refused to give any details to the public, but dental records confirmed details found on the driver's license. Positive identification, Conrad Sven Lindstrom. Libby's weekly newspaper, *The Libby Logger,* ran a special edition on Tuesday, a four-page tribute, announcing funeral services on Saturday. Norwegian flags joined American ones across town, flying at half-mast. Black cloth draped Libby's water tower and the hospital power station. Townspeople found their individual ways of mourning.

The pews in the small Episcopal church held 36 adults. Seventy people were allowed inside while hundreds gathered outside, standing or seated in folding chairs. A loudspeaker carried the sermon and short eulogies. Father Stjernholm seemed to enjoy upsetting Father O'Malley by speculating that Conrad might find his way to Valhalla to meet Thor and Freya face to face.

Instead of a coffin, in accordance with his final wishes, the doctor was laid to rest in a Morley cedar canoe, the red and blonde laminations practically glowing in the late afternoon sunshine. Conrad had picked up the canoe a few weeks earlier at the Morely workshop on Seeley Lake, storing it in the backyard shed. At the bow of the canoe, a small carved Viking dragon head seemed to laugh with a wide-open mouth. The canoe was wheeled outside, then pulled by a succession of loggers and miners, neighbors, patients and shopkeepers, down Montana Avenue, across Highway 2, and down Mineral Avenue, past the Blue Bear and the barber shop, past the shops, the drug store and movie theater. More and more people and half a dozen strangely subdued dogs joined the procession. Doc Conrad's two nurses pulled together, succeeded by a very old and unsteady Karl Swenson. Anna walked directly behind, in traditional Norwegian dress and apron. She wore her jade pendant, ring and earrings. Behind her, side by side, walked Nicholas and Trygve and their wives. Between them padded Andrew, the latest Lindstrom basset in a long line of Conrad's favorite breed. The procession passed the old post office and gas station at the end of Mineral Avenue, continuing across the railroad tracks to the banks of the Kootenai.

At sunset, the Kootenai appears to flow directly into the setting sun, the turquoise waters now glowing orange. Hundreds of 12-inch 2 x 6 pine boards were neatly stacked on the shoreline, produced in the lumber mill's box factory. Hundreds of votive candles filled three long folding tables, Father O'Malley's contribution. What happened next was strictly forbidden. Some say people in authority were unaware or looked the other way. I know better. The sheriff and four Kootenai National Forest rangers stood nearby as Nicholas and Trygve piled cedar branches onto the canoe, laced the branches with scented kerosene, draped a Norwegian flag on top, lit the branches and slid the flaming canoe into the river.

The canoe slipped obediently into the current, dragon head pointing toward the setting sun, flames reaching higher and higher. Behind the canoe, hundreds upon hundreds of lit votive candles began their journey, riding on wooden planks and following the now blazing canoe.

The front page of Sunday's *Libby Logger* pictured the canoe passing under the bridge followed by a tiny flotilla of twinkling lights, with Tryg's enigmatic caption, *as he fleeith afore, fainting I follow.* You can still see the photo at Libby's Lincoln County Library, along with 18 paint by numbers paintings that the Lindstrom family donated from Conrad's office.

23

Return to Kingfisher Creek (Tryg, age 27)

Great love is born of great knowledge of the thing loved.

Leonardo da Vinci

Tryg's nightmares began shortly after the funeral. At first, he was a young boy chased by wasps. He tried to run away but could only move in slow motion. The wasps grew larger and larger, stinging him and laughing. Several grabbed his clothing and began lifting him off the ground. Tryg awoke with a violent jerk, bathed in sweat and coughing. He sat up in his old bedroom. Mother was downstairs, now sleeping alone. Tryg planned to spend a week at home before returning to Harvard. Nicholas, now Dean of Faculty in the engineering department, had already returned to Purdue. Tryg looked around the bedroom, somehow cold without his books and journals, his shells and pinecones and wasp nests. He wondered if his mother would sell the house and downsize to something smaller.

The nightmare resurfaced. He was again being chased, this time by hissing cockroaches. Although he knew the insects were harmless (he kept a few in a terrarium in his classroom), the hordes were terrifying. He awoke, coughing and struggling for breath, reaching for his rescue inhaler. His asthma had gotten much worse; time to start the prednisone. His doctor had warned him that stress could trigger his asthma and recommended a sedative, but Tryg adamantly refused any additional medications.

Two days later Tryg stayed up late reading, reluctant to face another disturbing assault. The nightmare began again, this time with spiders in pursuit, large black and yellow spiders, orb weavers! They chased him down a trail into a deep wood, trees closing in on both sides. He alternately ran and floated down the narrowing path. Ahead he saw a terrifying image: a dense web blocking the path! If he continued running, he'd plunge directly into it. If he stopped, the spiders would be on him. He tried to turn off the path, but branches and thorn-covered vines grabbed at him. He awoke, gasping for breath. He sat up in bed, struggling for each breath. The rescue inhaler offered little relief. Maybe he should call 911. Two days ago he had started another course of prednisone, but it usually took three or four days for him to feel the effects. He should have started the medicine sooner when he had started coughing incessantly.

He stood up, unsteadily, took a step, pausing to breathe, then another small step and another long pause, finally reaching his nebulizer. The last thing he wanted was to wake his mother. For a moment he felt light-headed, fearing he might pass out. What would happen then? He filled the device with two ampules of albuterol sulfate, plugged in the machine and began inhaling the vapor. The cold steam seemed to help as he inhaled as deeply as he could. He had to face facts: his asthma was getting worse, alarmingly worse. His dour rheumatologist had bluntly warned that asthma could be serious, even fatal.

Fifteen minutes later, the last drops of albuterol were gone. Tryg was breathing a bit easier. He decided he'd stay home. If he went to the hospital, he knew they'd admit him, subject him to prednisone injections and periodic nebulizers, blood draws and maybe even a catheter. He'd give the prednisone one more day. He shuffled back to bed, praying for an undisturbed sleep.

When he awoke the next morning, the first thing he noticed: he was breathing! Full delicious breaths! By midnight that day, procrastinating going to bed, nursing his second mug of hot milk, he dozed off fearing another unnerving dream sequence. It came. This time the pursuers were two men, dressed in camouflage, carrying black automatic rifles. Overhead a military helicopter hovered with a loud *chop, chop, chop*, as Tryg ran through the dense forest. The men jogged behind him relentlessly, laughing as Tryg tried to escape. Why the mocking laughter, Tryg asked himself. The laughter seemed so ominous, so cruel. What do these men want? Leeches began crawling onto the trail; undulating ribbons of black flesh armed with a horrific circle of sharp white teeth. They covered the trail; Tryg had to run over them, slipping and falling, then curled into a ball awaiting his fate, leeches swarming over his body. He jerked awake, both calves cramping painfully.

Enough! He had to get away. Since he wasn't due back at Harvard for another week, he knew exactly where he had to go. Everything he needed was stored in the garage. He embraced his mother, telling her he'd be back in a couple of days and headed West on Highway 2 for about ten miles, pulling off at the place he remembered where his parents had dropped him off at age 16. He was surprised to see another car parked on the side of the road. Probably someone picking huckleberries, he thought. He locked the car and shouldered his backpack, making sure his grandfather's bamboo flyrod was safely secured in the short aluminum case.

Soon the road noises faded away as he entered the trail, familiar even though it had been more than a decade since he had made the trek. When Tryg arrived at the cedar forest, he dropped his pack and fished out a warm flannel shirt. Even on the warmest summer days the air was cool and damp in the cedar forest. He lay on his back at the base of an ancient tree and watched puffs of clouds through the few openings in the canopy. The ground was soft with centuries of cedarfall and the murmuring nearby creek lulled him into a deep sleep. He awoke with sunshine on his face, chilled but refreshed. He estimated he'd been asleep for three or four hours--oh how lovely to enjoy dreamless sleep.

Time to continue. He made good progress with strong strides, thankful for normal breathing, even when the trail ascended. Soon he stopped to stow his warm shirt, drinking deeply from his water bottle.

He began to regret that he hadn't packed a lunch or even a thermos of coffee, but he'd certainly enjoy fresh rainbow trout with his small supply of food he had brought for dinner: a potato, bacon and eggs to be cooked over an open fire. When he turned the final bend to see the waterfall, the deep grasses, the beaver ponds and Kingfisher Creek, the aspen and spruce, the wildflowers and butterflies, he felt the lifting of an invisible weight. Without warning he wept. His father's death had been no surprise. When the family had gathered to make preparations, Conrad had described his condition: lung cancer, emphysema, recent coughing of blood, both lungs failing. Each family member had accepted, respected and approved Conrad's decision. But from that moment Tryg had found it impossible to feel anything other than a stoic numbness.

Until this moment. He wept: great gulping, vocal cries, wave upon wave. He emptied himself, bending at the waist and dropping to his knees. He allowed Kingfisher Creek and the waterfall, the deep grasses and the woods, the warm sun, the larkspur and Indian paint brush, the beaver ponds and the circling osprey, he let them all embrace him. He surrendered to their care. His emotional numbness was replaced by a kaleidoscope of emotions and father-memories: the fishing trip on the Madison; the excursion to the Smithsonian; his father's enthusiastic, endearingly mediocre cello-playing; that his infectious laughter; killing wasps in the cabin with a broom. He was able to feel deep sadness, missing his father, but also grieved for the pain his mother and brother must be feeling. Why didn't they *talk* about such things? Emotionally drained, physically exhausted, he walked into the valley, deciding to set up his camp in the same spot he had chosen those many years ago.

It was now late in the afternoon. Tryg was hungry! Why hadn't he at least packed his usual hiking supply of trail mix and beef jerky? He'd love a meat loaf sandwich and a mug of strong coffee. Tryg got to work, quickly setting up his dome tent, rolling out his sleeping bag and then gathering a large supply of dry wood. The next person would certainly appreciate his surplus wood. By now the sun was low on the horizon--time to catch dinner. He opened the flyrod canister and tenderly lifted four short sections of his aged bamboo fly rod from the soft flannel sleeve. He decided on his favorite fly, a royal coachman (Nicholas wouldn't approve) and headed to the stream, carrying his single can of Moose Drool beer which he placed in the river to cool.

He waded into the water, welcoming the shock as sudden cold gripped his muscled bare calves and lower thighs. He stood in the strong, icy current that nearly reached his cargo shorts, knees bent, and began casting toward the far shore. The trout were just beginning to feed and Tryg soon began catching 10- and 12-inch rainbows. He thrilled to watch them leap again and again as he reeled them in, carefully releasing each one, expecting to land a "keeper" for an evening feast. He waded slowly upstream until he arrived at a promising deep hole. His cast sailed to the far bank, landing in the deep grass. Laughing at himself, he gently tugged the line, hoping the barbed fly wouldn't get snagged. He knew Nicholas would have placed his cast perfectly. Fortunately, the hook slid cooperatively through the grass and the coachman dropped from the bank into the pool.

Wham! The trout must have been lying in wait. The fish bolted straight downstream, Tryg's reel spinning. Tryg moved to shallow water and followed downstream, excited to feel the powerful tug of a big trout. As he came around the bend he reached the familiar huge logjam, his favorite kind of fishing spot. Fish congregate in the deep whirlpool in front of the logs. Wily trout head straight for the logs to snag the line, break the leader and pull free. It doesn't take much to snap a four-pound leader, and big trout seem to know just what to do.

Sure enough, his "keeper" (and potential dinner) headed straight into the deep pool, leapt completely out of the water, splashing heavily and then dove deep into liquid darkness. The tip of his rod bending perilously, Tryg played the fish carefully, always aware that his grandfather's ancient bamboo rod might be fragile. Then Tryg saw her. *Her!* Someone was sitting on *his* logjam. A woman! Fishing in *his* river. A fisherwoman! A stranger had intruded into his emotional sanctuary. Tryg felt an unaccustomed wave of anger.

The woman, startled by the unexpected kerplunk of Tryg's leaping trout, stood up quickly, saw the stranger and began losing her balance. First, one of the logs moved. Then both her feet slipped forward, and she began falling backwards in slow motion, landing on her backpack resting beside her. Still holding her flyrod, she and the backpack splashed into the river. For a second, Tryg kept playing his fish, unwilling to risk losing it; but the woman was up to her neck in icy water, her backpack bobbing and starting to sink as it moved downstream. He had no choice but to rescue the damn damsel in what might be genuine damn distress. At the very least she'd be weighed down by wet clothes. If she had worn waders, she could be in dire straits.

He laid his rod on the ground and waded in, barely able to keep his footing in the chest-deep water, wrapped an arm around her waist and pulled her to safety, releasing her on the shore and then splashing into the stream again to recover the sinking, waterlogged backpack. Drenched woman safely on the shore, Tryg returned to his rod. The trout was long gone. Both Tryg and the damsel were now soaking wet, dangerously chilled and shivering, and it was starting to get dark. Nothing to do but quickly get back to the campsite and light a fire. Tryg guided his guest to his campsite, instructing her to get into the tent, take off all her clothes and put on whatever warm clothing she could find in his backpack. Her spare clothes, sleeping bag and backpacking tent were completely soaked. She was already shaking and showing signs of hypothermia.

Meanwhile Tryg quickly started the campfire. By the time the intruder joined him, the fire was starting to take hold. She made her grand entrance wearing his athletic socks, sweatshirt and sweatpants comically much too large for her. She kept one hand on the waist to keep the sweatpants from falling. She was still shaking with cold, looking miserable, her hair dripping wet. Tryg couldn't help himself; he broke out laughing. To his surprise, she joined in the laughter.

The woman apologized profusely for losing his fish and sat close to the fire trying to warm herself. Tryg made a makeshift clothesline from his fly line, hanging up jeans, panties, bra, blouse, socks and tennis shoes. Tryg was now feeling the cold. He took off his wet shirt, shoes and socks, put on his flannel shirt and field jacket and sat by the fire barefoot in wet cargo pants. When he stopped shaking, he hung her sleeping bag and the rest of her wet gear on tree branches. They both hunkered down by the now roaring fire.

"I have a little food with me: three eggs, a potato and two slices of bacon," Tryg said. "And half a dozen Bit-o-Honeys for dessert. Hungry?"

"Starved," she replied, soaking up the warmth of the fire.

"Afraid I don't have any trout," Tryg said, suddenly aware his comment might be considered inconsiderate.

She got up and unstrapped the wicker creel from her backpack. "Will these do?" she asked with a big grin, holding up a pair of nice rainbows on a stringer.

While she warmed herself by the campfire, Tryg walked down to the stream to clean the fish. Then, using a strip of bacon to grease his aluminum backpacking pan, he sliced the potato, added salt and pepper, cracked open the eggs and the couple enjoyed a royal feast of pan-fried potatoes, scrambled eggs, trout and hot chocolate that the fisherwoman produced from a thermos in her backpack. For dessert, they each had three Bit-o-Honeys. Then he remembered the Moose Drool. They shared the rich brown ale as the Milky Way painted the sky, Tryg later enjoying saying he wouldn't trade that feast for prime rib and raspberry flambee at his favorite restaurant in Spokane.

"You sleep in the tent tonight," he said. "I insist. I'll sleep by the campfire."

For the first time Tryg took a good look at the woman who finally introduced herself as Moira. Her face glowed in the light of the fire and what a beautiful face it was. She wasn't at her best, dressed in oversized clothes that didn't exactly flatter her figure, auburn hair now sprouting in random directions like a haystack. She felt a bit guilty but thankful to be sleeping in Tryg's sleeping bag and tent.

They talked late into the night by the fire. The Milky Way blazed across the sky on a moonless night. The waterfall purred in the background. Tryg liked to say that she had been mesmerized by his culinary skills and Norwegian charm. Moira claimed she had simply given in to necessity. Even the hottest summer days turn into chilly nights on the Kingfisher; and without socks, Tryg's feet kept getting cold. He also had to get out of the wet cargo shorts, so he grabbed a dry pair of underwear from his backpack, adding his wet shorts and underwear to the clothesline. Moira finally said goodnight, Tryg insisting again that she use his tent. Tryg felt alternatively resentful of Moira's comfort and self-congratulatory for his exemplary nobility. He sat by the fire until dawn, watching the crescent moon rise. When early morning finally bathed the campsite in warming rays, Moira emerged. She looked at the makeshift clothesline and laughed. Her jeans and polo shirt were still damp, but the clothes had warmed in the sun and she managed to put them on for their hike back down the mountain.

The next day, Tryg sent Moira a ballad. He hoped he'd be able to sing it to her someday, accompanied by his baritone ukelele.

Oh come with me through wooded hills,
Through cedar hills and pine,
Beside the quiet river shore,
And I'll declare you mine.
Oh come through wooded hills, my dear
And I'll declare you mine.

The summer breeze is soft and warm;
The grasses down as feather,
And if you grant me but one kiss,
I'll ask thee for another.
Among the summer breezes soft
I'll ask thee for another.

The river sings to you and me,
Her pools are dark and deep;
So let us lie beneath the clouds
And we will fall asleep.

JIM NELSON

The river sings to you and me
And we will fall asleep.

Oh we will dream a laughing dream
While shadows long and longer.
I'll weave a garland for your hair,
As our love grows still stronger.
We'll share a laughing dream, my love
As our love grows still stronger.

Five months later they were married.

24

Jackson's Dog
(Tryg age 65)

The real voyage of discovery consists not in seeking new landscapes, but in having new eyes.

Marcel Proust

The Blue Bear Bar and Grill had six handles for the beers on tap: Bud, Bud Light, Coors, Coors Light, Miller, Miller Light. That's what the locals drank; that's what the owner provided. Pity the stranger who dared to ask for a porter or brown ale, an *import* or, God forbid, an IPA. No way in hell was Andy going to sell beer from India. "Grill" meant hamburger or cheeseburger or a grilled cheese sandwich, inevitably flavored with hamburger grease. Andy, proud owner and bar tender, pointed out his hand-painted sign to strangers: "Don't ask for French fries: This is America!" Pedestrian at best, the Blue Bear had one distinction that rendered it special: the freezer of frosted glass mugs and pitchers. No cheap plastic or warm mugs for Andy who was considering another sign: "Beer, served ICE-COLD: This is America!"

Olie Jackson rotated on his barstool to face a room of familiar faces. Strangers seldom visited the tired town. The vermiculite mine had closed down years ago. The once-thriving K. Swenson Lumber Mill was now a sort of self-serve museum, a cluster of derelict wooden buildings housing rusty relics of the sawmill. A massive five-foot-tall steel saw blade displayed four-inch teeth. Photos of logging trucks carrying huge cedars. One shed, dedicated to taxidermy, featured local fish (One had the label "squawfish" crossed out and "northern pikefish" written in black marker). There were stuffed birds and a standing black bear with missing claws. Even the museum was tired and ignored.

Half the stores on Mineral Street were closed; the Corner Drug was now a thrift shop; Ingebretson's Work Clothes now read "Pawn and Quality Used Guns." Remnants of daily commerce had gravitated to the edge of town where a strip mall featured a gas station/convenience store, Montana state liquor store, hardware/fishing tackle outlet and a Dairy Queen. Even the Texaco station at the end of Mineral Street was boarded up.

Tired. Libby was tired. Jackson was tired. For half a century Olie had driven a logging truck, six days a week. Then the mill closed. Just like that. A thousand employees suddenly out of work. A thousand families faced bills they couldn't pay. Hundreds of homes posted "For sale" signs within a month. Out-of-town realtors set up temporary offices in hopes of a windfall, but the homes didn't sell. Home prices plummeted. Many people owed more than their depreciated home values. People packed up and left. Let the bank have the damn place!

Some were marginally more fortunate than others. At least they owned their homes or trailers outright. Still, real estate was worth half of last month's value and prices continued to decline. Then the second shoe dropped. The sawmill had not only closed; it was bankrupt. Gone was the pension workers had funded year after year. Without a pension, more people left, homes unsold, to find any kind of work. Swenson moved his family, left the big house on the hill with swimming pool and tennis court. The big house, unsold, joined other empty homes.

Jackson began talking to no one in particular. His favorite topic: lamenting the lumber mill's closing. "How could they close the mill? People still need telephone poles and logs for cabins, don't they? They still need wooden boxes and lumber. Hell, *everyone* needs wood. Am I right? How can you build a house without wood?"

No one answered. Jackson's words were so completely ignored they simply faded into white noise of other conversations. For that matter, Jackson hadn't expected an answer as he continued his reminiscences punctuated by what he felt were urgent and poignant rhetorical questions. Other patrons sat at tables enjoying a cold brew. They had grown accustomed to tuning out or tolerating Jackson's rambling from his usual lonely barstool. Locals filtered into the Blue Bear Bar and Grill by twos and threes, occupying most of the tables on a Friday night.

"The Blizzard" was his best story. Wait long enough on a Friday night and he'd be sure to tell it. In the "blizzard of the century," some two dozen logging trucks sat idle as six feet of snow fell in one day! Yet Jackson made a courageous (foolhardy?) run up Turner's Mountain, eased six huge logs onto his trailer himself with the front-end loader at the site, and managed to slide down Thompson's Hill and Highway 2 without jackknifing.

"Sixty mile a 'nour, the wind," he'd say, lowering his voice dramatically. "Gusts up to 80! Couldn't see past 10 feet. Trees on both sides helped me stay on the road. Sure as hell didn't want to end up in a drift! Thirty below, it was. Deadly wind chill factor. Spit in the wind and the spit'd make a loud crack as it froze in the air." For some reason, he always laughed at this point as if he had just told a fine joke.

His rig had pulled through the lumber mill gate just as they were closing down Friday morning, the only day the mill had ever closed for weather. Highway 2 had just been closed from Kalispell all the way to Bonners Ferry. Half a dozen millworkers threw ugly epithets at Jackson when the foreman ordered them to measure and unload the oversized ponderosas and then dump them in the pond before punching out for the day. Jackson just sat in his cab laughing. The next week Karl Swenson himself slipped Jackson a $50 bill!

Jackson drained his mug. He always had a beer, then Andy delivered another fresh frosty mug with his cheeseburger. It was an old habit. When Nancy was still alive, he'd come to the Blue Bear every Friday night while Nancy and the "girls" met for their potluck and two tables of bridge. After his burger and second beer, Jackson liked to announce, "Gotta get back to the little woman."

Just as the bartender was about to collect a mug from the freezer and put in Jackson's usual order, Jackson stood, left some money on the bar and left early, noticing, somehow for the first time, that he was had been the only single in the place. Two or three people sat together at the tables, the barstools, empty. A wave of undefinable sadness washed over him.

What a fool I must seem, he mused. What am I doing rambling on to absolutely no one? They must think I'm senile. Hell, maybe I am! As Jackson walked into the warm moonless night, the bartender called, "G'night, Jackson." Without turning, Jackson waved.

His trailer was only a few blocks away. Each step felt as if he had lead weights in his shoes. As he walked, he admitted to himself, maybe for the first time, that he felt lonely. He had no children or grandchildren, no "buddy" to join him to watch a football game on the television, no siblings. He sat alone every Friday night at the bar. Now he was going home to an empty trailer.

Leaving the Blue Bear behind, Jackson trudged into darkness. The town had never installed streetlights. Half the homes he passed were long since abandoned. As he approached his humble home, pale porch light as his guide, he noticed a white bundle lying in front of the trailer door. His pace quickened and the bundle moved! It was a dog. A big white shaggy dog, with a wolf-like face. Jackson stopped. He tried to assess his own emotions. Was he afraid? Curious? Cautious? Jackson watched the dog's face for signs. The creature's ears perked up; that was promising. The dog's tongue hung to the side; he was panting gently--no snarl and show of teeth, no low menacing growl.

A great feathered tail began wagging. Jackson took another cautious step. More wagging. The dog watched the man alertly. Jackson knelt several feet away from his visitor and patted his leg. The great white shaggy wolf-like dog got up and trotted to the man. Jackson reached out and buried his hand in the thick, soft fur of the dog's neck. He realized his heart had been racing. The beast seemed calm, even friendly. He stood up slowly, still unsure of the dog's temperament.

He'd hate to feel those jaws tearing into his flesh.

Jackson walked calmly to the trailer door, the dog matching him step for step, eagerly looking up at Jackson as if waiting for a command. Jackson stopped and quietly said, "Sit." The dog sat. "Down." The dog lay down. "Sit." The dog got up and sat. "OK, Whitey, you're smart and someone has trained you. I guess you're not going to attack me. Might as well come in." Jackson opened the door and held it open. The dog didn't move. "In," Jackson commanded, and the shaggy beast entered Jackson's humble abode.

Jackson went to his refrigerator and looked for something a dog could eat. He supposed he could scramble some eggs. Did dogs like eggs? He settled on the last two wieners. He broke off small pieces and Whitey licked each piece gently from Jackson's open palm. Water. He must be thirsty. Jackson filled a soup bowl of water and watched with pleasure as Whitey lapped noisily. When Jackson sat down on the sofa, Whitey settled down with is head resting on Jackson's feet.

What to do? Whitey was obviously someone's dog, well cared for and trained. Someone must be looking for him. "Come," Jackson commanded, getting up and stepping outside. Whitey followed. Jackson decided to return to the Blue Bear, walking briskly now with a great white dog at his side. His heavy boots now felt light as sport shoes. His renewed entrance at the town's only bar created quite a stir as two women rushed over, kneeling down to pet the dog. The men all started talking at once. Jackson and his companion were suddenly centers of attention.

"Where'd you get the dog, Olie?"

"What kind is he?"

"Not a 'he,' dummie, it's a girl dog."

"Looks like one 'a them Great Pyrennes."

"Naw--he--I mean she, she's not wide enough."

"Has a German Shepherd face."

"Yeah, but German Shepherds aren't white."

"Some are."

"No way."

"It's some kind of mutt--looks like part wolf. Wolf dogs can't be trusted ya know."

"How ya going to find the owner? Somebody for sure is going to want their dog back."

"Ya gonna keep her?"

"Mebbe someone dumped her off at the edge of town. Mebbe they was tryin' ta get rid of her."

"She should have a collar . . . and a leash."

Suddenly the bartender interrupted the chatter. "Jackson," he said gently, "you can't have a dog in here. Sheriff'll close me down. Pretty sure that's not your *service* dog," he chuckled. "But seriously, you've got to take the dog outside."

"OK, Andy. But wouldja fry up a hamburger patty for--guess I need to give her a name. I've been calling her Whitey."

"One hamburger patty coming up," Andy replied. "And Whitey's a stupid name, Jackson, especially for a bitch."

"I don't like that word, Andy," one of the female patrons objected. Andy gave a sheepish shrug.

A few moments later Andy handed Jackson a brown paper bag.

"One rare hamburger patty for your . . . girl dog."

Friday night, two weeks later.

Jackson entered the Blue Bear ordered a beer, and sat down at an empty table.

"Hey Jackson," one of the men called out. "You still got that furry wolf dog." How 'bout joining my wife and I?"

"No thanks," Jackson replied. Then after a long pause, he said, "Well, maybe I will at that. Thanks for the invite."

Pretty soon, Jackson was telling the young couple how he had posted signs all over town about a lost dog and praying that nobody would respond. "I'm gosh-darned fond of that dog," he admitted. He beamed describing her brand-new red leash and collar, her dog dish and water dish and how he had bought a 40-pound sack of Dr. Ross Dog Food-- the good stuff. He often took Nancy. "That's her name," he said. "Same name as my wife, God rest . . . ." How he took Nancy with him fishin.' How Nancy barked and barked whenever he caught a trout. How he reckoned that after two weeks, Nancy was his. Possession was 90 percent of the law, right? "Tonight, I'm celebratin'" he announced.

"Whatcha celebratin?'" the young woman asked.

Jackson leaned toward the couple at the table and said in a conspiratorial tone, "I took all the 'lost dog' signs down today."

Jackson sat at the table and listened to the young couple--how she was going to have a baby and about the breakfast and lunch café they had just opened on Mineral Street. They even had an espresso machine. The first espresso machine in town! "Cost a pretty penny, I'll tell you," Joseph said with obvious pride. "This town isn't dead yet. There's going to be a homemade ice cream shop opening next door. And some folks are moving here. Old Rogstad finally sold his cabin on the Yaak to a young couple, the Lindstroms. You just watch; this town's making a comeback. That's why we named our place The Phoenix."

Jackson promised to have breakfast there in the morning. "Be sure to try Jennifer's huckleberry pie," Joseph said.

"Nothing better than huck pie and scrambled eggs and a cappuccino for breakfast," Jackson laughed, finishing off his last bite of cheeseburger and draining his second beer. Andy set a brown paper bag next to the empty mug. "I got a new 'tradition,'" Jackson told the couple. "Every Friday, one of the ladies comes by to fetch Nancy. They let her lay down near them when they play bridge. I pick her up on the way home."

"See y'all next Friday," he announced. "Gotta get back to the little woman."

25

A New Adventure
(Tryg, age 65)

To the natural philosopher there is no natural object unimportant or trifling . . . a soap bubble . . . an apple . . . a pebble . . . . He walks in the midst of wonders.

John Hershel

Tryg sat on the back porch of his log cabin, facing the Yaak River, as the sky began to glow orange and pink. It was nearly 10 p.m., but the sky wouldn't be dark for half an hour. A flotilla of white pelicans floated into view and on the opposite shore, a pair of blue herons dipped for crayfish. He expected to see several whitetails emerging from the aspen seeking a refreshing drink. It was his little piece of paradise. He had always loved the pristine river that wound its way to the Kootenai near Troy and had dreamed of building a cabin there, but Montanans rarely sold the few river properties that were privately owned. Most of the Yaak flowed through the Kootenai National Forest.

When the Realtor had finally called, Tryg had still been skeptical. Would the land be too close to the main road? Would there be cabins too close to his property? But as soon as he saw the property with the deep grass meadow and the cozy secluded cabin, he knew he had found the perfect place. The parcel was nearly 20 acres of riverfront where the Yaak meandered slow, clear and deep. Charlie Rogstad finally agreed with his children that he was too old to live alone an hour's drive from the nearest town. He had agreed to move to Kalispell, close to his three grandchildren. But Rogstad knew the value of his property and had refused to consider lower offers. With a wince, Tryg had agreed to the full asking price, unwilling to take a chance on losing it.

Retired at 70, Tryg still looked 35.

The porch door opened, and he was joined by a beautiful young woman who looked about Tryg's age. The pure white Kuvasz, Thor, padded beside her and sat expecting a treat. The woman sat next to her husband. "Here's your iced tea," she said, "and a cinnamon roll. I still can't make them like your mom did."

"Your cinnamon rolls won the blue ribbon at the Lincoln County fair. They are perfection!" Tryg admired the tjghtly-spiralled delights, heavy with cinnamon and brown sugar and laced with Paulette's special almond-crème frosting. "I think your cinnamon rolls are just smidge better than Mother used to make." Tryg's comment earned Paulette's smile and a peck on his cheek.

"How would you like to float the river with me tomorrow?" Tryg asked. "We could put in at the bridge at The Little Dirty Shame and end up right here. I just happened to notice there's enough leftover meatloaf to make sandwiches and Thor always loves it when all three of us go together."

"You go ahead, dear. I'll drop you and Thor off in that disreputable little boat. I'm going to spend the day finishing the quilt for our grandson."

"Time we paid my son, and grandson, another visit," Tryg answered. "Maybe we should drive to Denver next week."

"Next week!" Paulette laughed. "We just got back from Denver two weeks ago."

"I know, but little Lucas is changing so fast. And he's the only grandchild we've got. Maybe Erik and Ingrid should move to Libby."

Paulette laughed again, ignoring Tryg's familiar complaint. "Catch me a couple of trout, tomorrow," she said. "I'll barbecue them for dinner."

Suddenly Thor stood, ears laid back, giving an ominous growl.

"Way too late for the postman. Sounds like we have company," Thor said. "I'll go out front and see. C'mon Thor."

Tryg walked out the front door with Thor obediently complying with the "heel" command, just as two black Chevy Suburbans parked side by side on the front lawn in front of the cabin. Even the vehicle windows were tinted black, reminding Tryg of a pair of giant ground beetles. Thor shielded his eyes until the headlights went out.

Tryg noticed the U.S. Government license plates. "Oh no," Tryg groaned. "This must have something to do with Paulette," he thought.

Four front doors opened simultaneously as four men in dark suits and dark glasses emerged.

All four approached Tryg, flashing some kind of identification. The one holding a manilla envelope said simply, "CIA, we're to talk to Paulette Lindstrom and Dr. Trygve Lindstrom.

Thor growled again, baring ominous fangs.

"Down," Tryg commanded. The dog lay down, head raised, wary and alert.

All four men stopped. Tryg took in the scene, which he found comic. Four tall, athletic men dressed in black suits, each with a short haircut, ties that must have come from the same rack at the same store, impenetrable dark glasses, despite the growing darkness. Tryg was tempted to say something about looking up "stereotype" in the dictionary, but was aware of Paulette standing behind the screen door. Tryg, comfortable in cargo shorts, sandals and a white polo shirt, finally, spoke. "It's still 85 degrees on the Yaak river. We're 50 miles from the nearest town. And you come dressed like the Secret Service in D.C? Whoever's in charge, let me see your identification."

One man advanced, obviously wary of Thor who seemed under control, but without a restraining collar and leash. Thor quietly said, "Watch." The man hoped "watch" meant something like "be good," or "don't attack." Tryg looked carefully at the ID. "OK, Senior Agent Whitney. I'd like all of you to take off your jackets and ties, unbutton the top button of your crisp white shirts, and come into my humble abode."

Senior Agent Whitney frowned for a moment, shrugged and took off his suit coat and tie, his actions mimicked by his fellow agents. All four wore automatic pistols under their coats.

"Put the guns in your vehicles, boys. I'm pretty sure we're all friends here."

"Sorry, Dr. Lindstrom, Whitney responded. "We always go armed when on duty."

Thor stood, ears laid flat. "Sit," Tryg commanded. Thor sat, still baring his teeth. "Goodbye, gentlemen. Try calling next time.

"Heel." Tryg turned around, Thor at his side and began walking toward the door.

Just then the screen door opened. "Hello boys," Paulette said. "I've been listening for a few minutes and just made a call to a friend of mine. Senior Agent Whitney, my friend would like to talk to you." She stepped out and handed Whitney the phone.

Whitney reluctantly took the phone from Paulette. "Senior Agent Whitney here. Please identify yourself. "Oh, yes sir! . . . Understood. . . . No, I wouldn't want that to happen! . . . Wilco! . . . You have my full cooperation. . . . Yes sir. Goodbye, sir."

In less than a minute, Whitney's demeanor had dramatically changed, drops of perspiration dotting his brow. "Assistant Director, Lindstrom," Whitney managed to spurt out. "I had no idea you actually know the director of the CIA. I've never even talked to him before. With your permission, my colleagues and I would respectfully like to ask for a few minutes of your time."

"Good call, Whitney." Tryg said. "Her next call could have been to POTUS. I'm pretty sure you wouldn't like that phone call."

"Now, now, boys." Paulette said, smiling. "Please call me Paulette. I've been retired for years. I'm eager for our friendly little hat. It must be something important if Barnacle Bill sent you. Put away your jackets and cannons and testosterone. I'll make a nice pitcher of lemonade. Better yet, maybe we should get out the single malt."

It was now Thor's turn to grimace. He generally reserved his single malt for very best friends. He and Thor didn't much care for the new arrivals.

Thor, come!" Paulette said. The dog entered the cabin as four men scrambled to put their jackets and weapons in the Suburbans.

"Lose the ridiculous dark glasses, too," Tryg added, holding the screen door open.

Four men complied without comment.

The six of them took their places at the oval table. Tryg was relieved that his four guests accepted lemonade. Paulette put out a plate of crackers and cheese and brought Tryg's ice tea from the back porch. Thor settled peacefully at Tryg's feet. The four men seemed to relax. Then it just happened. Paulette quietly took charge of the meeting.

"To the point, Whitney," she said. "It's late."

"Yes ma'am, er, Paulette. We're here to ask for your help--for you and Dr. Lindstrom and (he paused to take out a small notebook) someone named Mamba Oten."

"Croc!" Tryg exclaimed!

"Something terrible's happening along several tributaries of the Amazon. The NSA, The Director herself, personally, wants you, Paulette, to accept a temporary assignment. You'll have the authority of an Assistant Director, reporting directly to the Director. And she wants Dr. Lindstrom to join you, and this Mamba person who should be arriving in Chicago tomorrow. We're scheduled to pick him up in Kalispell the next day and instructed to bring him here."

"What exactly is our mission," Paulette asked?

"Apparently, we don't have a 'need to know.' A top-secret clearance isn't enough. Right now I feel like Director Barney's messenger. Did you actually call him 'Barnacle Bill'? All I'm supposed to do is show Professor Lindstrom these photographs," Whitney said, opening the envelope and laying four prints on the table. Just look like bugs to me. Well, "three bugs and a butterfly."

Tryg finally showed an interest. He studied each photo in silence. "Are these real?" he asked quietly.

Whitney shrugged.

"What's the matter, Tryg?" Paulette asked.

"Look at these insects," he answered. "*Acrocinus longimanus, Titanus giganteus. Dynastes hercules. Morpho cypris.* Something's terribly, terribly wrong. Each one has eight legs.

"We need to go the Amazon."

Milton Keynes UK
Ingram Content Group UK Ltd.
UKHW010637240424
441619UK00001BA/134